Goethe

Egmont

Goethe

Egmont

1. Auflage | ISBN: 978-3-75251-640-1

Erscheinungsort: Frankfurt am Main, Deutschland

Erscheinungsjahr: 2020

Salzwasser Verlag GmbH, Deutschland.

Nachdruck des Originals von 1868.

GERMAN CLASSICS.

Egmont.

Ein Schauspiel

von

Goethe.

ANNOTATED BY

E. A. OPPEN,

Of Haileybury College, Author of 'International German Reader,' &c. &c.

LONDON:
LONGMANS, GREEN, AND CO.
1868.

By the same Editor.

SCHILLER'S *WILHELM TELL*, price 2*s.* 6*d.*

'This is one of a series of German classics carefully edited from the latest German editions, and furnished with excellent Notes, well suited for English learners, especially those who have some knowledge of Latin. The Introduction gives a clear account of the circumstances on which the play is founded, and nothing is omitted which an intelligent student would be likely to require.' ATHENÆUM.

'The Editor has done his work conscientiously and thoroughly. The Play is preceded by an historical introduction, giving an account of the events on which *Wilhelm Tell* is founded, and referring especially to the sources from which SCHILLER derived his information. The Notes on the text seem to us remarkably good. Unusual words and phrases are lucidly explained, syntactical peculiarities are illustrated, and the results of comparative philology are often very appropriately introduced. Along with all this we have important historical notes.' MUSEUM.

'This neat and correctly-printed little volume forms one of a new series of German Classics, and the moderately advanced student of that language will be greatly assisted in comprehending the beauties of the original by the careful annotations of Professor OPPEN. These will save him from the irksome labour of constant reference to a dictionary, which, after all, could not guide him to the sense of any passage so clearly as it is here given. The pages of the book are, besides interspersed throughout with historical notices and references of great value; and altogether the series promises to be a very useful and excellent addition to our elementary publications.'

MIDLAND COUNTIES HERALD.

GOETHE'S *IPHIGENIE AUF TAURIS*, price 2s.

*** GOETHE's *Iphigenie auf Tauris* is the Play selected by the Cambridge Local Board for the subject of the Local Examinations in German in December 1868.

'*Iphigenie auf Tauris*, the second of the series of Standard German works edited for English learners by Professor OPPEN, is a tragedy well known to be one of GOETHE's masterpieces. It supplies very good reading for a pupil who has previously gone through such a play as SCHILLER's *Wilhelm Tell*, the same Editor's annotated edition of which we lately recommended. The *Iphigenie auf Tauris* shews traces of the same careful preparation observable in *Wilhelm Tell*. Such editions of annotated foreign classics are extremely valuable for advanced students.'

LONDON REVIEW.

'This is another of the series of German Classics which Mr. OPPEN is editing with English notes. The notes are calculated to remove the difficulties of English learners of German; they are judicious, strictly illustrative, and afford all the explanation needed. Mr. OPPEN prefixes an admirable introduction on the subject of the play. This play ought to be much read in classical schools, and affords good materials for comparing with the tragedy of EURIPIDES of the same name. Mr. OPPEN in his commentary applies this comparison to several passages, which appear to have been happily imitated by the German poet.' MUSEUM.

'An excellent school edition of GOETHE's admirable drama. The NOTES afford all necessary aid in rendering the more difficult constructions. In the INTRODUCTION, Professor OPPEN details the original legend, and discusses the modifications it has received under the treatment of the great German poet.'

EDUCATIONAL TIMES.

To follow immediately *in the same Series of* CLASSICS:—

LESSING'S *MINNA VON BARNHELM*, with English Notes.

LESSING'S *NATHAN DER WEISE*, with English Notes.

London: LONGMANS and CO. Paternoster Row.

LONDON: PRINTED BY
SPOTTISWOODE AND CO., NEW-STREET SQUARE
AND PARLIAMENT STREET

INTRODUCTION.

Lamoral, Count of Egmont, Prince of Gavere, Baron of Fiennes, the hero of this play, was born 1522, and derived his name and title of Egmont from an old castle, town, and lordship on the north-western side of the peninsula of North Holland. His ancestors had been independent sovereigns in Frisia, 'but, like other great houses, had paled in the lustre of the powerful Burgundian princes, and become faithful lieges of the Spanish descendants of that illustrious family.' He inherited his second title, Prince of Gavere, from his mother, Frances of Luxemburg, Princess of Gavere. In his early youth, he accompanied Charles V. in his Algerian expedition, commanding a troop of light horse, and gave promise of future eminence.

After his return, he was, in his twenty-third year, united to Sabina of Bavaria, sister of Frederic, Elector Palatine, in the presence of the emperor, of his brother Ferdinand, King of the Romans, all the Imperial Electors, and the principal nobility of Germany.

In the following year, 1546, Charles invested him with the order of the Golden Fleece, and selected him, in 1554, to be his ambassador to England, where he solicited for Philip the hand of Mary, daughter of Henry VIII., whose marriage he witnessed at Winchester Cathedral.

In 1557, the emperor entrusted to him, who was esteemed by many one of the foremost generals of the age, the important post of commander of the horse in the French campaign, in which capacity he joined the forces of the Duke of Savoy before St. Quentin, an important city on the Somme, defended by Admiral Coligny.

The choicest troops of the French, commanded by the Constable Montmorency, attended by princes of the blood, attempted to reinforce the city, but were only partially successful. The council of war held in Egmont's tent on the question whether a general engagement should be risked were swayed by Egmont's eloquent appeal, and finally determined to cut off the constable's retreat.

Egmont's keen eye had discovered the weak point in the enemy's line, viz. a narrow pass between two narrow hills, through which the French had to pass on their return, and he had, although it was occupied by the Rhinegrave, to whose assistance the Duke of Nevers had been hastily despatched by Montmorency, ordered 2,000 of his cavalry to occupy the gorge. The daring movement was quickly executed before the arrival of Nevers' four companies. The French army, retreating, approached this 'fatal pass,' whence issued Egmont with his cavalry, charging their left flank; while the Dukes of Brunswick, assisted by Count Hoorn, attacked their right, and Mansfeld, Hoogstraten, and Lalain burst upon their front. The rout was complete. Half the French troops lost their lives, the remainder were utterly dispirited and broken up. Of the generals, the Prince of Condé and the Duke of Nevers cut their way through the Spanish troops; the constable, wounded in the groin, was a prisoner, as well as the Dukes of Montpensier, of Longueville, the Prince of Mantua, the Rhinegrave; the Duke of Enghien was brought in mortally wounded, and expired shortly after. It is almost past belief that of Philip's army but fifty lost their lives, while the flower of the French chivalry was slain almost to a man.

'Such,' continues Mr. Motley, 'was the brilliant victory of St. Quentin, worthy to be placed in the same list with the world-renowned combats of Crecy and Agincourt; and from that day forth the name of the brave Hollander was like the sound of a trumpet to the army. "Egmont and St. Quentin" rang through every mouth to the farthest extremity of Philip's realms. The fame and power of the constable faded. On the other hand, the exultation of Philip was as keen as his cold and stony nature would permit. The magnificent palace-convent of the Escorial, dedicated to the saint on whose festival the battle had been fought, was soon afterwards erected, in pious commemoration of the event.'

The next achievement, crowning Egmont with glory, was the overthrow of the victorious Marshal de Thermes at Gravelines. He had forced the battle upon the French commander, who was returning from a successful raid, crowned by the burning of Dunkerk, and had for himself selected the post of danger in the front rank of his cavalry. His horse was shot under him. Mounting another, he cheered his men on to another attack. The battle was fierce; a long hand-to-hand fight; neither party yielding, when at last the English squadron appeared in the offing and fired upon the French. The moral effect, although the vessels were out of range, was instantaneous. The French ranks broke, never to reform. Horse and foot fled in wild confusion; many hundreds were slain, still more driven into the sea, and drowned, or, worse still, fell into the hands of the armed peasantry, who revenged themselves for the injuries inflicted by the once victorious army, and annihilated what the ocean and Spanish valour had spared.

Although the result of this battle was so glorious that it laid France helpless at Philip's feet, although Egmont became the idol of the army, praised and extolled in song and story, and was, in the expressive words of Mr. Motley, 'hailed throughout the Netherlands as the right hand of the fatherland, the saviour of Flanders from pillage and devastation, the protector of the nation, and the pillar of the throne,' yet to this battle, and the glory directly and indirectly resulting from it, must be ascribed his eventual ruin and fall, for he made one enemy, who was destined to be the instrument of his destruction, viz. the Duke of Alva, who had strongly advised against giving battle to De Thermes, and who indulged in sarcastic criticisms and reflections upon the results of a possible defeat. The victorious hero was unable to repress his anger at what he justly considered an envious detraction, and treated the duke, in the presence of the king, with an arrogance and hauteur which the proud Spaniard never forgot or forgave. The vengeance which he vowed for the insult he had received was sated on the day when he had seen his rival's head laid low.

Philip sent, upon the request of the French king, the Prince of Orange, Alva, Egmont, and the Duke of Aerschot to the French court, as hostages for the due execution of the treaty of Cateau Cambresis—a treaty of which Marshal Monluc wrote, 'that never a more disgraceful one had been ratified by a French monarch,' as no less than one-third of the whole monarchy was signed away by the king.

The unfortunate accident which befell the French monarch at the tournament, when he fell mortally wounded by Montgomery's lance, wrought a more disastrous change in the internal policy of that kingdom, and paved the way to negotiations between Philip and Henry III., son of Catherine de Medicis, which were carried on directly through the medium of the Duke of Alva, and had for their immediate object the extinction of Protestantism itself. Philip felt that his presence in the Netherlands would be not only superfluous, and that a regency would amply meet all exigencies, that he determined to leave for Spain, and appointed, much to the surprise of all, Margaret of Parma, the natural daughter of Charles V., who, in conjunction with a state council, consisting of the Bishop of Arras, the Prince of Orange, Count Egmont, Viglius, and Berlaymont, was to administer the affairs in the Netherlands. Count Hoorn, the admiral of the Provinces, was to be the resident minister in Spain. The real power of the council was placed in the hands of a consulta, that is to say, of the Bishop of Arras, for although both Viglius and Berlaymont formed part of it yet they were mere instruments in the hands of that astute prelate.

Before leaving, Philip took occasion to harangue personally the estates of the various provinces, both at Mechlin and Ghent, enlarging on the importance of their individual efforts to aid him in stamping out that most damnable heresy, Protestantism; omitting at the same time, what was most desired by his northern subjects, to mention the withdrawal of the foreign troops.

The estates had without murmur voted the extraordinary supplies demanded by the government; they all, however, made the withdrawal of the Spanish troops 'a condition antecedent to the payment of their respective quotas.' In addition to the verbal enunciation of the wishes of the people, a 'solemn remonstrance' had been drawn up, and signed by the principal nobility, including the Prince of Orange, Counts Egmont and Hoorn, and others, laying before his majesty a recital of the wrongs suffered by his dutiful subjects on the hands of the Spanish soldiery, stating particularly that the inhabitants of Marienburg and of many other large towns had voluntarily quitted their homes rather than remain and endure such insolence and oppression.

Although the request was most inopportune, and totally at variance with Philip's secret intentions, he yet felt that dissimulation was his best policy, as his plans were not yet matured; and he therefore replied, after an outburst of ill-temper, that the command of the foreign troops should be given to Count Egmont and the Prince of Orange, and that they should be withdrawn in three or four months. Nevertheless, he openly showed his displeasure at the course pursued by the nobility, and, when leaving the Netherlands, upbraided the Prince of Orange, and forgot himself so far as to shake him violently by the wrist and to use offensive and uncourteous language.

The choice of the Duchess Margaret was in many respects a fortunate one. She was, as observed above, the natural daughter of Charles V., the favourite monarch, by a Dutch lady, and had been brought up in the family of Hoogstraten, whence she passed into the care of her paternal aunt, Margaret of Savoy, and eventually into the household of the emperor's sister, Mary, Queen of Hungary. She had studied the principles of government in Italy, was versed in the Machiavellian school of politics, habitually industrious, and capable of supporting a great deal of fatigue. Two further recommendations she possessed, viz. an unbounded obedience and entire subjection to the will of the sovereign, and—the most valuable of all in the eyes of Philip and the Bishop of Arras (who directed Philip's choice)—she was a devout and enthusiastic Catholic, such as Loyola, who had been her confessor and guide, would look upon with delight.

Nor was her personal appearance without that 'grand and imperial fascination' belonging to the members of her family; and although she was in her person and tastes masculine, it would be difficult to point out anyone who so fitly represented Philip, or who so implicitly followed the dictates of that monarch. On the other hand, it would be vain to assert that, from her spiritual predilections, she was at all able to understand the Protestant movement, certainly not qualified to sympathise with the sufferings inflicted by the harsh edicts emanating from the Spanish court, and, finally, utterly incapable of either quelling the storm that was surely coming or of managing the conflicting interests so as to bring them into harmony with her own requirements.

The condition of the Netherlands at the outset of her

career was such as offered no small prospect of future grievous trouble. Commerce had suffered considerably, consequently everything else. Devastation and famine had followed in the wake of the ruinous contest with France. Taxes were heavy, and there was no definite chance of their ceasing soon. Worse than all, the great houses, who ought to have been the mainstay and support of the poor and needy, by their own extravagance had so far encumbered themselves as to be utterly helpless and incapable of assisting.

War, though bringing certain reward in the shape of ransom for the commander, had also its train of heavy expenditure, and it is very doubtful whether Egmont was not poorer after his successful career as a general than before. Of Orange, we know that, although he had married the richest heiress in the Netherlands, yet his debts amounted to very nearly a million florins. In spite of this general financial embarrassment, ostentation and display were at their height, bringing in their train gambling and excesses of all kinds. In short, the state of society in the upper classes was such as to give serious cause for apprehension; for not only did these excesses affect the highest in the land, but, like a cancer, spread ruin in every direction.

Indirectly, also, this decay favoured Protestantism. The church in the Netherlands was inordinately wealthy, and there can be no doubt that many of the ruined nobles looked upon the broad acres possessed by the religious communities, upon the wealth accumulated by centuries of thrift and economy, as a ready means of once more enabling them to continue a career of idleness and debauchery.[1] Hence they not only did not support the magistracy in their efforts to uphold the edicts of the king against the schismatics but they connived with the latter, favoured religious agitation in the hope of bringing about a general riot and revolt, by which they might profit.

The general discontent—kept up and fed daily by the excesses committed by the foreign soldiery, and, above all, by the horrible cruelties perpetrated here as elsewhere in that dark age of persecution by the misguided zeal of religious fanatics—was fanned at last into flame by the re-enactment of the edict of 1550, which forbade the reading of all writings of the Reformers, the holding of conventicles, the conversation or dispute of all laymen on the Holy Scriptures, all preaching and teaching, under the most severe penalties: for it provided that the men offending were to be executed with the sword; the women to be buried alive if they proved repentant, but, if they persisted in their errors, then they were to be executed with fire.

This proclamation, which had been borne patiently enough from the hands of the Emperor Charles in the year 1550, when promulgated afresh, ten years later, by Philip, on the instigation of the Bishop of Arras, coupled with the bull of Paul IV. on the increase of the episcopate (confirmed by Pius IV. in the next year), created a ferment and agitation which led eventually to open rebellion. In the second measure, which was viewed with, if possible, greater dislike than the first, Philip had not con-

[1] The wealth of the religious houses in the Provinces was very great. The abbey of Affighem alone had a revenue of 50,000 florins, and there were many others scarcely inferior in wealth. —*Motley.*

sulted the late Bishop of Arras, since become Archbishop of Mechlin, and better known under the title of Cardinal Granvelle; but the people attributed the bull to his influence, and although the king, upon a direct appeal from the cardinal, proclaimed both to the regent and other influential persons openly that there was not the least foundation for this report yet the people refused to give credence to this disclaimer, and the cardinal had to encounter an odium, on that account, which made him exclaim, 'Would to God these (the new bishoprics) had never been established!' The relations between the nobles and the cardinal became more and more difficult. On the one hand, he was, intellectually, and by position, as Philip's chosen friend and minister, superior to them; but, on the other, they looked down upon him on account of his obscure origin, and chafed under the restraint they were obliged to put upon their tempers. With Egmont especially the cardinal was on a very indifferent footing—so much so that Egmont on one occasion was with difficulty restrained from offering him personal violence; and the Prince of Orange, who also had to suffer from the cardinal's supercilious conduct in the council, went so far as to address a letter, signed by him and Egmont, to the king, entreating him to accept their resignation of the offices they held, or place them on an equal footing with the cardinal.

Philip's mind, however, was so far under the control of the wily churchman, who had represented to him that, in the matter of the bishoprics and the Inquisition, Philip's policy was continually being thwarted by the nobility, that he not only turned a deaf ear to all complaints but burst out into violent language to Count Hoorn, exclaiming,

'What, miserable man! you always complain of this cardinal, and always in vague language;' and wrote to the cardinal 'that the time for chastisement had come, as those rascals (the nobles) could only be made to do right through fear.'

From this moment, Philip's mind seems to have been fully made up. Though he might be obliged, from financial reasons, to temporise, though he might from political motives be induced to feign friendship and profess regard, he was too unbending, too unforgiving, too unscrupulous, not to satisfy his wrath sooner or later.

Of the persecution of the Protestants in the Provinces, though no doubt it was carried out to the letter of the edicts promulgated by the king, I have occasion to say less, as it is not so much connected with the play, indeed, mentioned but once (compare scene between Egmont and his secretary; Scene 2, Act II.). It needs only to repeat the statement made by Philip in a letter to the Regent Margaret, 'Wherefore introduce the Spanish Inquisition? That of the Netherlands is much more pitiless than that of Spain.'

The opposition to the cardinal by the nobles gradually extended. Philip, in answer to their letters, invited Egmont to come to Spain, to confer with him in person—an expedient, as he himself wrote to the Duchess of Parma, to gain time. This invitation Egmont, upon the advice of the Prince of Orange and Count Hoorn, declined; and the three nobles, finding their endeavours to gain a favourable consideration for their moderate requests eluded and thwarted by the king, withdrew at last trom the council, begging the regent to excuse their non-attendance. Margaret, who herself was by no means a friend of the cardinal, whom she had reason to suspect of double-dealing, despatched her private secretary, Thomas Armenteros, to Spain, to lay before his majesty the actual state of affairs in the Netherlands, stating that it would be impossible for her to continue the government, and that it might cause a revolt, were she to retain the cardinal in the Netherlands. Philip turned for counsel to the Duke of Alva, who advised him 'not to recall the cardinal, to administer flattery and deceitful caresses to Egmont, who would be more easily entrapped than the others.'

Of the famous dinner-party given, in December 1563, by the treasurer-general, Caspar Schetz, and the attempt made by Egmont to turn into ridicule the pompous display made by the cardinal's retainers, by inventing a new livery worn by the domestics of all the great noble houses, consisting of doublet and hose of the coarsest grey stuff, with long hanging sleeves, having a monks cowl embroidered on them in silver, I shall have occasion to speak in the historical note in the text. The cardinal's reign was all but over. Philip, after weighing maturely all the chances, had reluctantly given way, so far as to recommend to the cardinal a temporary withdrawal from the Provinces. The regent, drawn into closer union with the nobles, was rejoicing to be relieved of the presence of a man whom she had begun by liking very much and ended by hating bitterly, and of whom she was now sending most damaging statements to Philip, at the same time assuring the cardinal 'that she loved him like a brother.' The unpopularity which his arrogance had called forth outlived his fall; more than a year after his departure from the Provinces, Berlaymont is reported to have said 'that the nobles hated him now even worse than before, and would eat him alive if they caught him.'

'The remainder of the year,' says Mr. Motley, 'after the retirement of the cardinal was one of anarchy, confusion, and corruption.' Yet there seemed a time when the growing danger might have been averted had Philip been inclined to clemency. The persecution of the Protestants, however, was so truly devilish, the ingenuity of the tortures so exquisite, that the less courageous began to leave the country in numbers, and all agreed 'that it was better to die at once than to live in perpetual slavery.' The king was by the inquisitors Tiletanus and De Bay informed of the advance of heresy, and he urged upon the regent the necessity of greater severity, and more stringent measures, although she herself had written to him pressing letters concerning a revision of the edicts. The king, however, was not to be moved from his purpose. His answer was a peremptory command to use the utmost severity. The excitement grew in all quarters. Seditious placards were posted everywhere, calling upon the nobles to come forward and lead the people in a crusade against their hated oppressors. Meanwhile, the council, obedient to the behests of their master, prepared the proclamation ordering that the council of Trent, the *edicts* and Inquisition should be immediately published in every town and village, and once in six months for ever after. That decree was answered 'by a howl of execration.' 'Men high in authority sympathised with the general indignation,' and the four principal cities of Brabant drew up a formal protest and denunciation against the violation of their ancient charters. The result of their spirited stand was a complete victory. Brabant was declared free of the Inquisition. Nevertheless, the agitation continued to increase. Publications, handbills, placards, open letters were found daily and nightly in the streets, and affixed to the churches and the principal houses in the Provinces, exhorting the patriots to rise and strike the long-delayed blow, and though the marriage festivities of the union of Prince Alexander of Parma, son of the regent, with Dona Maria of Portugal, sent a temporary ray of joy and happiness over the scene, there was that in the air which foreboded the bursting of the volcano that lay smouldering and groaning under their feet.

On the very day this marriage was celebrated, Francis Junius, a preacher of the Reformed church, was haranguing an assembly of nobles at the Culenburg Palace, among them probably those who not long after pledged themselves in the '*Compromise*,' viz. Brederode, Mansfeld, and Count Louis of Nassau, a document which obtained signatures to the number of 2,000 and more within a few days. The language of the document was such that it could be signed by Catholics and Protestants alike. While it deplored the presence of strangers, who, by misguided zeal for the Catholic religion, led the king to violate the oaths which he had taken; it also declared 'the Inquisition to be iniquitous, contrary to all laws, human and divine, surpassing the greatest barbarism which was ever practised by tyrants,' and bound the signers by holy covenant and sacred oath to resist the Inquisition, and to 'extirpate the thing in any form, as the mother of all iniquity and disorder.'[2]

---

[2] It has been computed by the Prince of Orange, a man most likely to be well informed on such a point, that the Inquisition and the edicts had caused the death of no less than 50,000 persons.

The confederates, under the leadership of Count Brederode, asked permission of the regent to present to her a solemn request to be forwarded by her to the king, and although Berlaymont and others of the council to whom this demand was referred were of opinion that the readiest means of stifling the rebellion would be to invite the confederates in a body to the palace, and cut them down to a man, the Prince of Orange and others insisted that a friendly meeting and hearing ought to be accorded to gentlemen who were for the most part their own relatives and men of honour. It was finally decided to receive Count Brederode's deputation on April 3, 1566. More than 300 gentlemen preceded Count Louis of Nassau and Brederode into the senate chamber, where the latter read the covenant, filled indeed with protestations of loyalty to his majesty, yet worded precisely enough to show that the continuation of the edicts and the Inquisition would lead to a general rising. They concluded by imploring the regent to stay all further proceedings of the Inquisition until his majesty's pleasure should be known.

The duchess, overcome with agitation and in tears, replied that the matter should receive the immediate attention of her council, and she would give them the answer then decided upon.

It was on this occasion that Berlaymont uttered the famous speech which gave a name to the party of malcontents. He exclaimed, 'What, madam, you can be afraid of these beggars (gueux)?' The by-word was accepted by the confederates at a banquet given by their chief, who had a leathern wallet, such as was worn by professional beggars, and a wooden bowl brought to him, and putting the one round his neck, he drank out of the other to the success of the 'gueux.' A costume in harmony with the name was also invented, consisting of coarse grey doublet and hose, with short cloaks, slouched felt hats, and beggars pouches and bowls.

Meanwhile, the council were busy in drawing up a 'Moderation,' which after all substituted only another form of capital punishment for the stake, viz. the gibbet. No doubt this was a considerable boon. All the former edicts against the professors and teachers of the Protestant religion continued in force, or were re-enacted, so that the word 'moderation' was, except in the instance quoted above, a bitter sarcasm.

That no one needed the proclamation that the Protestant movement grew stronger daily is not to be wondered at. The people, having trust in their leaders, no longer concealed their persuasion. They boldly met in the fields, in armed bands, and listened to the eloquent appeals of their persecuted pastors; nor to them alone, for religious fury had come upon the people. The blood of the martyrs had borne fruit. The uneducated, the lowly, stood up and preached with tongues and words of fire, and called on the multitudes to withstand their common enemy. Though prizes, tempting to many, might be put upon the heads of the preachers Francis Junius, Ambrose Wille, Herman Strycker, Peter Datenus, and others too numerous to mention, the measure came too late. The persecuted had in their turn become pursuers. The wave of Protestant fanaticism—the iconoclastic fury—broke over the land, and, sweeping away the symbols of the dominant church, avenged years of persecution in the space of a few summer's nights. 'Pictures, statues, organs, ornaments, chalices of silver and gold, reliquaries, albs, chasubles, copes, cibories, crosses, chandeliers, lamps, censers, all of the richest materials, glittering with pearls, rubies, and other precious stones, were scattered in heaps of ruin upon the ground.'

In Antwerp, more than thirty churches were thus sacked in one night. In vain did the preachers of the Reformed faith inveigh against the senseless destruction, in vain did the magistrates implore the people to desist from outrages that would be certain to be avenged in the blood of the innocent; the rioters heeded no one. The tocsin sounded, and they rushed forth. Yet, to their honour be it said, no priest was murdered, no violence committed against individuals. Theft was rigorously punished by the rioters. Their object was to destroy, not to enrich themselves.

The successive reports which reached the regent of the excesses committed made a deep impression upon her. Though one cannot lay cowardice to her charge, one cannot help thinking that she actually apprehended that the end of her government had come, and that she had better provide for her own safety, and withdraw from the town. The counsel of the nobles, however, prevailed upon her to stop and face the peril. On August 25, she signed an agreement with Louis of Nassau, allowing freedom of preaching and liberty of worship, abolishing the Inquisition, and granting an amnesty for past events.

The great nobles departed, each for his seat of government, and earnestly set about the difficult task of bringing back peace and order: Egmont to Flanders, Orange to Antwerp, and Count Hoorn to Tournay—Orange alone with secret misgivings as to the sincerity of the promises made.

He felt that they were hollow, that preparations were being made for coercive measures, and resented especially the insult which had been offered to him by the regent's order to the Duke of Brunswick to occupy certain fortified towns in his province. He therefore tried several times to induce Counts Egmont and Hoorn to prepare in return to meet all sudden exigencies. With Egmont he failed. The reasons are not far to seek. Egmont's sympathies were with the Catholics; he himself was, if not a zealous, yet a warm adherent of the church. He also had no sympathy with the people at large. He was traditionally popular with them, not from any positive good that he had done for them. He was a staunch friend of the king—thoroughly loyal, even when opposing him—and if any disloyal thought ever crossed his mind, he quickly cast it aside from prudential motives. He had a large family; all his possessions were in the power of the king. On his side, he was a powerful noble; against him, but a poor unit in an army of poor malcontents.

With Count Hoorn, Orange succeeded better, because the count had his own special grievances against the emperor, against Philip, against the duchess, 'of whom he bluntly said, that he would no longer treat with ladies upon matters concerning a man's honour;' but although he might separate him from the government, he could not prevail upon him to meet actively the coming storm. He was, therefore, to a certain extent, paralysed, yet keeping an ever watchful eye on all movements of the king, even controlling the secret correspondence by means of his numerous spies.

The government, meanwhile, pressed vigorously the siege of Valenciennes, and the cruelties perpetrated by the infuriated bigoted soldiery against the unhappy peasantry shadowed forth faintly what was impending over the doomed city, who had called upon the confederates for help, and even addressed a letter to the knights of the Golden Fleece, in the vain hope of rousing sympathy in their hearts by a recital of their sufferings. Brederode, indeed, attempted a diversion by peremptorily calling upon the regent to disband the forces which had been collected, and to uphold in good faith the 'August' treaty. He received a contemptuous reply, added to the hint that he had better go back to his home and rest in peace, lest the regent should be tempted to make an example of him. The troops, amounting to 3,000, which had been collected by Marnix of Tholouse, brother of St. Aldegonde, at Ostrawell, were cut down to a man by the commander of the regent's body-guard, Philip de Lannoy, assisted by 400 Walloons, supplied by Egmont.

Happening as it did within sight of Antwerp, this event roused the anger of the Calvinistic section; and but for the bold decisive action of the Prince of Orange, who managed to hold them in check by the attitude of the Lutherans and Catholics, the town would have been a prey to civil war. Valenciennes, summoned to surrender by Egmont and Aerschot, still held out, preferring rather to undergo the very worst than accept the terms proposed by the government. Noircarmes, following the advice of Egmont, bombarded the 'White Tower,' and the city surrendered, after the first day's cannonade, on condition that the lives of the inhabitants should be spared, and no sack be permitted. Notwithstanding this promise, many hundreds of the principal citizens were beheaded, and 'for two whole years there passed hardly a week in which several were not executed!'

The success of the royal armies elated the government so much that the regent imposed a new oath upon all in high stations, civil and military, as well as the knights of the Golden Fleece, 'to yield unqualified obedience to *all* the commands of the king.' Brederode angrily refused. Orange declined politely, stating that he had been true to his old oaths, and there was therefore no need to take a new one. Mansfeld, Egmont, Aerschot, Berlaymont, took it at once. Hoogstraten, Count Louis of Nassau, Culenburg, Berg, joined Orange.

The memorable interview between Orange and Egmont altered nothing in their mutual position as regards the oath. Egmont steadfastly remained loyal, 'speaking with confidence of the royal clemency.'

The confederacy was entirely broken up; the leaders were either in exile, in prison, or dead, and when Orange departed for Germany, 'the country was absolutely helpless, the popular heart cold with apprehension. All persons implicated in the late troubles or suspected of heresy fled from their homes.'

The mere rumour of what turned out to be a sad truth made the Protestants fly from the Netherlands; the tranquillity so much desired by Philip had at last come; no preaching of schismatic fanatics, armed to the teeth, could be heard; the Catholic Church was everywhere triumphant, and needed no longer the strong arm of the Spanish soldiery to protect it from insult and harm. The pontiff, however, who was not aware of the fact, had sent a special envoy to Philip, to rate him for the remissness he had shown, and the lack of energy displayed in his dealings with the Protestant heresy; added to this rebuke, there was in the council one who urged the monarch to persevere with his chastisement, in the hope of being himself selected as instrument. The Duke of Alva, rumours of whose coming had long preceded his appointment, was at length commanded by Philip to lead a select army into the Provinces. No one could be fitter for that task. Of the march and the army I have spoken elsewhere.

Margaret was deeply mortified when the news of the coming appointment of the duke reached her. She besought his majesty to think twice before he sent another Spanish army into the Provinces, which she had succeeded in quieting. Philip also, in his letter to the princess, is very careful not to let her see the full extent of his plans, especially as he had just then heard from her that 'the name of Alva was so odious in the Netherlands that it was enough to make the whole Spanish nation detested.' She received the duke in a manner which must have shown him how cordially she disliked him. Of this, however, he took no notice. He had no object in openly quarrelling with her. Besides, the instructions of his royal master would, he felt sure, sooner or later relieve him of the necessity of further interviews.

Already many of the nobles had left the palace, and come over to the Culenburg mansion to pay their respects to the new rising star, who 'strove by brilliant amusements and festivities to dissipate the gloom' which had fallen upon Brussels when the news of his approach had spread. He followed in all these proceedings the dictates of Philip, with whom he had previously concerted the plan for action.

Counts Egmont and Hoorn were taken prisoners on September 9, at a meeting of the council of state in the Culenburg palace. Previous to their arrest, Egmont's secretary, Backerzele, and Van Stralen, the burgomaster of Antwerp, an intimate friend of the Prince of Orange, had been secured.

The prisoners were subsequently removed to Ghent, as the safest of the strongholds in the Provinces. A new tribunal, with extraordinary powers, was installed to investigate the causes of the late outbreak. It was composed of twelve judges, 'les plus savants, les plus intègres du pays et de la meilleure vie.' Amongst them, conspicuous for the vile subserviency with which they obeyed the secret dictates of their chief, must be mentioned Juan de Vargas, Del Rio, and Hessels, besides Berlaymont and Noircarmes.

Of the illegality of all proceedings in this court, called into existence by the bare wish of the Duke of Alva, without warrant from the sovereign, against all usage and privileges of the Provinces, it is needless to say much. The trial of the Counts Egmont and Hoorn was most deliberate, if not dilatory. Backerzele, Egmont's secretary, had been put to the torture several times, but not even the rack had been able to extract from his lips what might have been construed into an admission of guilt. Personal interrogatories were then resorted to, and laid the foundation for the accusation, drawn up by Du Bois. In it Egmont was charged with having conspired with others, William of Orange notably, to shake off the Spanish rule and divide the government among themselves. He was further accused of having encouraged the schismatics. Of heresy he could not have been accused by the most exacting of priests; it was, however, laid to his charge that he regarded the holy Inquisition with contempt and detestation. The charges against Count Hoorn were similar; both gentlemen admitted certain facts, and denied the rest. 'Such,' continues Mr. Motley, 'were the leading features in these memorable cases of what was called high treason. Trial there was none. The tribunal was incompetent; the prisoners were without advocates; the government evidence concealed; the testimony for the defence was excluded; and the cause was finally decided before a thousandth part of its merits could have been placed under the eyes of the judge who gave the sentence.' The king's signature to the death-warrant had come over with Alva. The prisoners were, on June 3, 1568, brought back from Ghent to Brussels, and on the following day, 'Alva declared before God and the world that he had examined the documents,' and pronounced their doom. At the same time, he sent for the Bishop of Ypres, and commanded him to communicate the sentence to the prisoners, and prepare them for death. The task was a painful one. The bishop vainly besought Alva to spare the lives of the two nobles until the king's pleasure was known, and at last about midnight was ushered into Egmont's room, whom he found fast asleep. He bore the news calmly; after ascertaining the fact that the sentence was irrevocable, he wrote to the king, testifying his loyalty, and beseeching his majesty to care for his sorrowing widow and children.

During the night the preparations for the execution had been made in the great square, where Egmont, 'in happier days, had often borne away the prize of skill or valour, the cynosure of every eye, and hence, almost in the noon of life, illustrated by many brilliant actions, he was to be sent, by the hand of tyranny, to his great account.'

At eleven o'clock Julian Romero arrived at the Broodhuis, where Egmont and Hoorn were confined, and conducted the former to the scaffold. Egmont's bearing was noble. He chanted on his way the fifty-first Psalm; arrived on the scaffold, he said the Lord's Prayer aloud, and requested the bishop to repeat it three times. He then kissed the silver crucifix, knelt down, folded his hands, and cried, 'Lord, into Thy hands I commend my spirit.' The head fell at a single blow. . Count Hoorn was executed immediately afterwards.

This is the brief outline of the historical portion of the play. I have followed Motley's and Prescott's accounts, as well as Gachard's and Schiller's narratives. The play itself was written in the years 1775–77, following 'Götz von Berlichingen,' which was written in 1772, and 'Werther,' written the year after.

I have retained the original text, preferring it to Schiller's arrangement. The historical allusions will be found explained in the foot-notes. Of the touching character of Clärchen, I will remark merely that she is not altogether a creation of the poet's fancy; her real name was Joan Lavil, and the shock sustained by her at the sight of her lover's execution broke her heart.

It is impossible to conclude this introduction without ample reference to William of Nassau, Prince of Orange. The ancestors of this powerful noble—the elder branch of whose house had ascended the imperial throne in the thirteenth century, in the person of Adolf of Nassau—had begun to exercise sovereignty in the Netherlands four centuries before the advent of the house of Burgundy. That overshadowing family afterwards numbered the Netherland Nassaus amongst its most staunch and powerful adherents. Engelbert II., a distinguished general and counsellor of Charles the Bold, supported Maximilian with equal fidelity. He was succeeded by his brother John, whose two sons, Henry and William, divided their vast patrimony; William, taking the German estates, became Protestant, and introduced the Reformation into his dominions. Henry, the elder, received the family titles and possessions in Luxemburg, Brabant, Flanders, and Holland, and distinguished himself greatly in the service of the Burgundo-Austrian house. He was the confidential friend of Charles V. In 1515, he married the sister of Philibert of Orange, Claudia, and his son, Réné de Nassau-Chalons, succeeded Philibert. At the death of this prince (1544, in the trenches of St. Dizier), all the titles and estates went to his cousin-german, William of Nassau, son of his father's brother William, who thus at the age of eleven became William IX. of Orange. He was especially fortunate to have the care of a most exemplary and pious mother, Juliana of Stolberg, and much of the high-mindedness and uprightness of character so eminently evinced by the son is directly ascribable to her influence. At an early age, he was sent into the emperor's family as page, and Charles V., a keen judge of human nature, at once recognised the more than common abilities of the boy, whom at the early age of fifteen he treated more as a friend than a subject. He was present at all councils, and he acquired in consequence a more than ordinary insight into public affairs, a precocious development of unusual talents. At the age of twenty-one, he was appointed general-in-chief of the army on the French frontier, a post desired by many distinguished soldiers—among them by Count Egmont—and the result justified the emperor's choice. It was he on whose shoulders the emperor leaned, October 25, 1555, in the chapter-room of the Golden Fleece, in Brussels, at the solemn occasion of the abdication, and he who bore the imperial insignia to Ferdinand at Augsburg; but among the great triumphs of his early years—he was barely of age—must be reckoned the treaty of Cateau Cambresis, signed April 1559, concluded with France.

No less great was the diplomatic skill which he evinced when the King of France, after the conclusion of the treaty, made known to him the scheme formed by the two monarchs, Philip and Henry, for the suppression of Protestantism. A permission, granted him soon after this memorable interview, to visit the Netherlands, gave him the opportunity, so much desired by him, to agitate at once for the removal of the Spanish regiments, on whose help both monarchs counted as the readiest means in their projected massacre, and to the command of which Egmont and himself were subsequently appointed. Yet it would be a perversion of historical truth to suppose that he was at this time, 1559, the distinguished champion of Protestantism which we find him in later years. He was still a Roman Catholic, though not one professing undue zeal, occupying himself rather with the political than the religious aspect of the position of affairs in his country, and it is not overstating the fact when we conclude that his eventual conversion was due to the gradual development of Protestant ideas, added to the political exigencies of the time, and most of all to his union with the Protestant Princess Anne of Saxony. With William of Orange, an unwillingness to serve as instrument in the hands of the Spanish monarch was the result rather of chivalrous high-toned motives than a strong religious conviction. He was in his youth too fond of pleasures, disposed for a luxurious, easy, pleasant life. His household was on a princely scale; he had twenty-four noblemen and eighteen pages of gentle birth continually with him; he kept open house, and his tables were daily filled with numbers of welcome guests. That such a mode of living entailed an expenditure far beyond his means cannot be doubted, and although he had followed the traditions of his house in marrying, 1551, the richest heiress in the Netherlands, Anne of Egmont, who died as early as 1558, yet we find that his debts amounted to very nearly a million florins.

After his marriage with the Princess Anne of Saxony, his religious views changed considerably. 'Sincerely and deliberately a convert to the Reformed church, he was ready to extend freedom of worship to Catholics and Anabaptists alike.' He was as firm as pious; self-denying and lavish of his resources for others.

As a military commander he was famous; esteemed by many even Alva's equal. He ranks, if possible, higher as a politician. From the very outset in his political career, he exercised a rare prudence and caution, discerning the machinations of his enemies before they had even matured their own plans. He possessed no mean share of eloquence, and exercised a powerful sway over his hearers. Added to this, he had a memory that neither 'forgot an event nor a face.' It is not the place here to enter into a disquisition of the various estimates that have been formed of his character. Party feeling will often reproduce aspersions that are difficult to prove or disprove. For our purposes the above delineation of his character will suffice to understand the scene in the text (Act II. Scene 3). For ampler information and a more detailed account, the reader is referred to the volumes of Prescott, Motley, and Gachard.

Egmont.

Personen.

Margarete von Parma, Tochter Carls des Fünften, Regentin der Niederlande.

Graf Egmont, Prinz von Gaure.

Wilhelm von Oranien.

Herzog von Alba.

Ferdinand, sein natürlicher Sohn.

Machiavell, im Dienste der Regentin.

Richard, Egmonts Geheimschreiber.

Silva, }
Gomez, } unter Alba dienend.

Clärchen, Egmonts Geliebte.

Ihre Mutter.

Brackenburg, ein Bürgerssohn.

Soest, Krämer, }
Jetter, Schneider, }
Zimmermann, }
Seifensieder, } Bürger von Brüssel.

Buyck, Soldat unter Egmont.

Ruysum, Invalide und taub.

Vansen, ein Schreiber.

Volk, Gefolge, Wachen u. s. w.

Der Schauplatz ist in Brüssel.

Erster Aufzug.

Erste Scene.

Armbrustschießen.[1]

Soldaten und Bürger mit Armbrüsten.

Jetter, Bürger von Brüssel, Schneider, tritt vor[2] und spannt[3] die Armbrust. Soest, Bürger von Brüssel, Krämer.

Soest. Nun schießt nur hin, daß es alle wird![4] Ihr nehmt mir's doch nicht! Drei Ringe schwarz, die habt ihr eure Tage[5] nicht geschossen. Und so wär' ich für dies Jahr Meister.

Jetter. Meister und König dazu. Wer mißgönnt's euch?[6] Ihr sollt dafür auch die Zeche doppelt bezahlen; ihr sollt eure Geschicklichkeit bezahlen, wie's recht ist.

Buyck, ein Holländer, Soldat unter Egmont.

Jetter, den Schuß handl' ich euch ab,[7] theile den Gewinnst, tractire die Herren: ich bin so schon lange hier und für viele Höflichkeit Schuldner. Fehl' ich, so ist's, als wenn ihr geschossen hättet.

Soest. Ich sollte drein reden:[8] denn eigentlich verlier' ich dabei. Doch, Buyck, nur immerhin.

Buyck (schießt). Nun, Pritschmeister,[9] Reverenz! — Eins! Zwei! Drei! Vier!

Soest. Vier Ringe? Es sei!

---

[1] **Armbrustschießen,** shooting-match. The word **Armbrust,** arbalist, crossbow, seems to be derived from **Arm** and **Rüst,** weapon for the arm.

[2] **tritt vor,** steps forward.

[3] **spannt,** bends.

[4] **daß es alle wird,** that there is an end.

[5] **eure Tage,** all your life.

[6] **mißgönnt's euch?** grudges it.

[7] **handl' ich euch ab,** buy it of you.

[8] **sollte drein reden,** ought to protest; **nur immerhin,** go on.

[9] **Pritschmeister,** marker; also buffoon; so called from **Pritsche,** 'a bat,' or wooden sword, like the one used by the clown on the stage.

Alle. Vivat, Herr König, hoch! und abermal hoch!

Buyck. Danke, ihr Herren. Wäre Meister zu viel! Danke für die Ehre.

Jetter. Die habt ihr euch selbst zu danken.

Ruysum, ein Friesländer, Invalide und taub.

Daß ich euch sage![10]

Soest. Wie ist's, Alter?

Ruysum. Daß ich euch sage! — Er schießt wie sein Herr, er schießt wie Egmont.

Buyck. Gegen ihn bin ich nur ein armer Schlucker.[11] Mit der Büchse trifft er erst, wie keiner in der Welt. Nicht etwa wenn er Glück oder gute Laune hat; nein! wie er anlegt,[12] immer rein schwarz geschossen.[13] Gelernt habe ich von ihm. Das wäre auch ein Kerl, der bei ihm diente und nichts von ihm lernte. — Nicht zu vergessen,[14] meine Herren! Ein König nährt seine Leute; und so, auf des Königs Rechnung, Wein her!

Jetter. Es ist unter uns ausgemacht,[15] daß jeder —

Buyck. Ich bin fremd und König und achte eure Gesetze und Herkommen nicht.

Jetter. Du bist ja ärger als der Spanier; der hat sie uns doch bisher lassen müssen.

Ruysum. Was?

Soest (laut). Er will uns gastiren; er will nicht haben, daß wir zusammenlegen, und der König nur das Doppelte zahlt.

Ruysum. Laßt ihn! doch ohne Präjudiz! Das ist auch seines Herrn Art, splendid zu sein, und es laufen zu lassen, wo es gedeiht.[16]

(Sie bringen Wein.)

Alle. Ihro Majestät Wohl! Hoch!

---

[10] Daß ich euch sage, As I tell you.

[11] Gegen ihn bin ich nur ein armer Schlucker, I am, compared with him, but a poor wretch.

[12] wie er anlegt, whenever he aims.

[13] immer rein schwarz geschossen, he always hits the bull's-eye.

[14] Nicht zu vergessen, ere I forget.

[15] unter uns ausgemacht, agreed amongst ourselves.

[16] es laufen zu lassen, wo es gedeiht, lit. to let it run out, to be generous, open-handed, where it is profitable.

Jetter (zu Buyck). Versteht sich Eure Majestät.

Buyck. Danke von Herzen, wenn's doch so sein soll.

Soest. Wohl! Denn unserer spanischen Majestät Gesundheit trinkt nicht leicht ein Niederländer von Herzen.[17]

Ruysum. Wer?

Soest (laut). Philipps des Zweiten, Königs in Spanien.

Ruysum. Unser allergnädigster König und Herr! Gott geb' ihm langes Leben.

Soest. Hattet ihr seinen Herrn Vater, Carl den Fünften, nicht lieber?

Ruysum. Gott tröst' ihn! Das war ein Herr! Er hatte die Hand über den ganzen Erdboden und war euch alles[18] in allem; und wenn er euch begegnete, so grüßt' er euch, wie ein Nachbar den andern; und wenn ihr erschrocken wart, wußt' er mit so guter Manier — Ja, versteht mich — Er ging aus, ritt aus, wie's ihm einkam,[19] gar mit wenig Leuten. Haben wir doch alle geweint, wie er seinem Sohn das Regiment hier abtrat — sagt' ich, versteht mich — der ist schon anders, der ist majestätischer.

Jetter. Er ließ sich nicht sehen, da er hier war, als in Prunk und königlichem Staate. Er spricht wenig, sagen die Leute.

Soest. Es ist kein Herr für uns Niederländer. Unsre Fürsten müssen froh und frei sein, wie wir, leben und leben lassen. Wir wollen nicht verachtet noch gedrückt sein, so gutherzige Narren wir auch sind.[20]

Jetter. Der König, denk' ich, wäre wohl ein gnädiger Herr, wenn er nur bessere Rathgeber hätte.

Soest. Nein, nein! Er hat kein Gemüth gegen uns[21] Niederländer, sein Herz ist dem Volke nicht geneigt, er liebt uns nicht; wie können wir ihn wieder lieben? Warum ist alle Welt dem

---

[17] trinkt von Herzen, drinks heartily, willingly.

[18] war euch alles. The euch is purely colloquial, and remains untranslated.

[19] wie's ihm einkam, or einfiel, as it came into his head.

[20] so gutherzige Narren wir auch sind, although we are but good-natured fools.

[21] kein Gemüth gegen uns, has no sympathy with us.

Grafen Egmont so hold?[22] Warum trügen wir ihn alle auf den Händen? Weil man ihm ansieht, daß er uns wohl will; weil ihm die Fröhlichkeit, das freie Leben, die gute Meinung aus den Augen sieht; weil er nichts besitzt, das er dem Dürftigen nicht mittheilte, auch dem, der's nicht bedarf. Laßt den Grafen Egmont leben! Buyck, an euch ist's, die erste Gesundheit zu bringen! Bringt eures Herrn Gesundheit aus.

Buyck. Von ganzer Seele denn: Graf Egmont hoch!

Ruysum. Ueberwinder bei St. Quintin![23]

Buyck. Dem Helden von Gravelingen![24]

Alle. Hoch!

Ruysum. St. Quintin war meine letzte Schlacht. Ich konnte kaum mehr fort, kaum die schwere Büchse mehr schleppen. Hab' ich doch den Franzosen noch eins auf den Pelz gebrannt, und da kriegt' ich zum Abschied noch einen Streifschuß ans rechte Bein.[25]

Buyck. Gravelingen! Freunde! da ging's frisch! Den Sieg haben wir allein. Brannten und sengten die wälschen Hunde[26] nicht durch ganz Flandern? Aber ich mein', wir trafen sie! Ihre alten handfesten Kerle hielten lange wider,[27] und wir drängten und schossen und hieben, daß sie die Mäuler verzerrten und ihre Linien zuckten.[28] Da ward Egmont das Pferd unter dem Leibe niedergeschossen, und wir stritten lange hinüber herüber, Mann für Mann, Pferd gegen Pferd, Haufe mit Haufe, auf dem breiten flachen Sand an der See hin. Auf einmal kam's, wie vom Himmel herunter, von der Mündung des Flusses, bau, bau! immer mit Kanonen in die Franzosen drein. Es waren Engländer, die unter dem Admiral Malin von ungefähr von

---

[22] so hold, so fond of.

[23] Ueberwinder bei St. Quintin! conqueror at St. Quentin. *Vide* Introduction.

[24] Dem Helden von Gravelingen! hero of Gravelines.

[25] kriegte ich noch einen Streifschuß ans rechte Bein, I received a grazing shot in my right leg.

[26] die wälschen Hunde, the foreign dogs.

[27] hielten lange wider, i.q. leisteten lange Widerstand, withstood a long while.

[28] ihre Linien zuckten, their lines wavered, lit. quivered.

Dünkirchen her vorbeifuhren.[29] Zwar viel halfen sie uns nicht; sie konnten nur mit den kleinsten Schiffen herbei, und das nicht nah genug; schossen auch wohl unter uns — Es that doch gut! Es brach die Wälschen und hob unsern Muth. Da ging's! Rick! rack! herüber, hinüber! Alles todt geschlagen, alles ins Wasser gesprengt. Und die Kerle ersoffen, wie sie das Wasser schmeckten; und was wir Holländer waren, gerad hintendrein. Uns, die wir beidlebig[30] sind, ward erst wohl im Wasser wie den Fröschen; und immer die Feinde im Fluß zusammengehauen,[31] weggeschossen wie die Enten. Was nun noch durchbrach, schlugen euch[32] auf der Flucht die Bauerweiber mit Hacken und Mistgabeln todt. Mußte doch die wälsche Majestät gleich das Pfötchen reichen und Friede machen. Und den Frieden seid ihr uns schuldig, dem großen Egmont schuldig.

Alle. Hoch! dem großen Egmont hoch! und abermal hoch! und abermal hoch!

Jetter. Hätte man uns den statt der Margrete von Parma[33] zum Regenten gesetzt!

---

[29] Engländer, die unter dem Admiral Malin von ungefähr von Dünkirchen vorbeifuhren. The incident is described by Motley in the following words:—'For a long time, it was doubtful on which side victory was to incline, but at last the English vessels unexpectedly appeared in the offing, and, ranging up soon afterwards as close to the shore as was possible, opened their fire upon the still unbroken lines of the French. The ships were too distant, the danger of injuring friend as well as foe too imminent, to allow of their exerting any important influence upon the result.'

[30] beidlebig, amphibious.

[31] zusammengehauen, i. e. wurden, were cut down.

[32] euch; colloquial, untranslated.

[33] Margarete von Parma was the natural daughter of Charles V., and had been brought up by her aunt, Margaret of Savoy, and the emperor's sister Mary, Queen-Dowager of Hungary. Only twelve years of age, she was forced to marry Alexander de' Medici, and when after a few months of a miserable married life the assassination of her husband set her free, she lived for some years at her father's court, and at the age of twenty married Ottavio Farnese, the nephew of Paul III., then only thirteen years of age. Her youthful husband accompanied the emperor in his expedition to Barbary, and was subsequently created Duke of Parma and Piacenza. At the age of thirty-seven,

Soest. Nicht so! Wahr bleibt wahr! Ich lasse mir Margareten nicht schelten. Nun ist's an mir.[34] Es lebe unsre gnäd'ge Frau!

Alle. Sie lebe!

Soest. Wahrlich, treffliche Weiber sind in dem Hause. Die Regentin lebe!

Jetter. Klug ist sie und mäßig in allem, was sie thut; hielte sie's nur nicht so steif und fest mit den Pfaffen.[35] Sie ist doch auch mit schuld, daß wir die vierzehn neuen Bischofsmützen im Lande haben.[36] Wozu die nur sollen? Nicht wahr, daß man Fremde in die guten Stellen einschieben kann, wo sonst Aebte aus den Kapiteln gewählt wurden? Und wir sollen glauben, es sei um der Religion willen. Ja, es hat sich.[37] An drei Bischöfen hatten wir genug: da ging's ehrlich und ordentlich zu. Nun muß doch auch jeder thun, als ob er nöthig wäre; und da setzt's[38] allen Augenblick Verdruß und Händel. Und je mehr ihr das Ding rüttelt und schüttelt, desto trüber wird's. (Sie trinken.)

Margaret, who had been carefully schooled in the Machiavellian art of politics, was singled out by Philipp II. on account of her reputed talents, her energy, and her zeal in the interests of the Roman Catholic Church, for the office of nominal regent in the Netherlands, the real ruler being Anthony Perrenot, Bishop of Arras, subsequently known under the title of Cardinal Granvelle.

[34] Nun ist's an mir, Now it is my turn.

[35] hielte sie's nur nicht so steif und fest mit den Pfaffen, were she only not so firmly attached to the priests.

[36] die vierzehn neuen Bischofsmützen im Lande haben. Up to the year 1559, there had been but four sees in the Netherlands, viz. Arras, Cambray, Tournay, and Utrecht, the first three being under the supervision of the Archbishop of Rheims, the latter under the control of the Archbishop of Cologne. By the bull of Paul IV., dated May 18, 1559, confirmed by Pius IV., in January following, three archbishoprics were appointed, viz. Mechlin, Cambray, and Utrecht, the first exercising jurisdiction over the new sees of Antwerp, Bois-le-Duc, Roermont, Ghent, Bruges, and Ypres; Cambray, over Tournay, Arras, St. Omer, and Namur; and Utrecht, over Haarlem, Middleburg, Leeuwarden, Groningen, and Deventer.

[37] Ja, es hat sich, Not a bit of it.

[38] da setzt's, there are.

Soest. Das war nun des Königs Wille; sie kann nichts davon, noch dazu thun.[39]

Jetter. Da sollen wir nun die neuen Psalmen nicht singen;[40] sie sind wahrlich gar schön in Reimen gesetzt und haben recht erbauliche Weisen. Die sollen wir nicht singen; aber Schelmenlieder, so viel wir wollen. Und warum? Es seien Ketzereien drin,[41] sagen sie, und Sachen, Gott weiß. Ich hab' ihrer doch auch gesungen; es ist jetzt was neues, ich hab' nichts drin gesehen.

Buyck. Ich wollte sie fragen![42] In unsrer Provinz singen wir, was wir wollen. Das macht, daß Graf Egmont unser Statthalter ist; der fragt nach so etwas nicht. — In Gent, Ypern, durch ganz Flandern singt sie, wer Belieben hat. (Laut.) Es ist ja wohl nichts unschuldiger, als eine geistlich Lied? Nicht wahr, Vater?

Ruysum. Ei wohl! Es ist ja ein Gottesdienst, eine Erbauung.

Jetter. Sie sagen aber, es sei nicht auf die rechte Art, nicht auf ihre Art; und gefährlich ist's doch immer, da läßt man's lieber sein. Die Inquisitionsdiener[43] schleichen herum und passen auf; mancher ehrliche Mann ist schon unglücklich geworden. Der Gewissenszwang[44] fehlte noch! Da ich nicht thun darf, was ich möchte, können sie mich doch denken und singen lassen, was ich will.

---

[39] kann nichts davon, noch dazu thun, can neither take away from nor add to.

[40] die neuen Psalmen nicht singen. Clement Marot's (1495–1544) Protestant version of the Psalms, introduced from France, and set to music by Theodor de Bèze, 1563.

[41] Ketzereien darin, full of heresy. Ketzerei, derived from the Italian *gazzari*, i. q. *puritan*.

[42] Ich wollte sie fragen! I would not ask their leave.

[43] Inquisitionsdiener, servants of the Inquisition; originally established by Ferdinand the Catholic and Pope Alexander VI. for the Moors and Jews in Spain. Under the first inquisitor-general, Torquemada, 8,800 individuals were burned alive, 6,500 in effigy, 97,321 punished with imprisonment, banishment, confiscation of property, and the like. It was a court owning allegiance to no temporal authority, was without appeal, arrested on mere suspicion, tortured until confession, and punished by fire.

[44] Gewissenszwang, oppression of men's consciences.

Soest. Die Inquisition kommt nicht auf.[45] Wir sind nicht gemacht, wie die Spanier, unser Gewissen tyrannisiren zu lassen. Und der Adel muß auch bei Zeiten suchen, ihr die Flügel zu beschneiden.

Jetter. Es ist sehr fatal.[46] Wenn's den lieben Leuten[47] einfällt, in mein Haus zu stürmen, und ich sitz' an meiner Arbeit, und summe just einen französischen Psalm, und denke nichts dabei, weder Gutes noch Böses; ich summe ihn aber, weil er mir in der Kehle ist; gleich bin ich ein Ketzer und werde eingesteckt.[48] Oder ich gehe über Land[49] und bleibe bei einem Haufen Volks stehen, das einem neuen Prediger zuhört, einem von denen, die aus Deutschland gekommen sind; auf der Stelle heiß' ich ein Rebell und komme in Gefahr, meinen Kopf zu verlieren. Habt ihr je einen predigen hören?

Soest. Wackre Leute. Neulich hörte ich einen auf dem Felde vor tausend und tausend Menschen sprechen. Das war ein ander Geköch,[50] als wenn unsre auf der Kanzel herumtrommeln und die Leute mit lateinischen Brocken erwürgen.[51] Der sprach von der Leber weg;[52] sagte, wie sie uns bisher hätten bei der Nase herumgeführt, uns in der Dummheit erhalten, und wie wir mehr Erleuchtung haben könnten. — Und das bewies er euch alles aus der Bibel.

Jetter. Da mag doch auch was dran sein. Ich sagt's immer selbst und grübelte so über die Sache nach.[53] Mir ist's lang' im Kopf herumgegangen.

Buyck. Es läuft ihnen auch alles Volk nach.

Soest. Das glaub' ich, wo man was gutes hören kann, und was neues.

---

45 kommt nicht auf, cannot, or will not, thrive.

46 fatal, disagreeable.

47 lieben Leuten; ironical.

48 eingesteckt, put in prison.

49 gehe über Land, go into the country.

50 ein ander Geköch, other, different, fare.

51 die Leute mit lateinischen Brocken erwürgen, choke people with bits of Latin.

52 sprach von der Leber weg, spoke out boldly; did not mince matters.

53 grübelte nach, pored over.

Jetter. Und was ist's denn nun? Man kann ja einen jeden predigen lassen nach seiner Weise.

Buyck. Frisch, ihr Herren![54] Ueber dem Schwätzen vergeßt ihr den Wein und Oranien.

Jetter. Den nicht zu vergessen. Das ist ein rechter Wall: wenn man nur an ihn denkt, meint man gleich, man könnte sich hinter ihn verstecken, und der Teufel brächte einen nicht hervor. Hoch! Wilhelm von Oranien, hoch!

Alle. Hoch! hoch!

Soest. Nun, Alter, bring' auch deine Gesundheit.[55]

Ruysum. Alte Soldaten! Alle Soldaten! Es lebe der Krieg!

Buyck. Bravo, Alter! Alle Soldaten! Es lebe der Krieg!

Jetter. Krieg! Krieg! Wißt ihr auch, was ihr ruft? Daß es euch leicht vom Munde geht, ist wohl natürlich; wie lumpig aber unser einem dabei zu Muthe ist,[56] kann ich nicht sagen. Das ganze Jahr das Getrommel zu hören; und nichts zu hören, als wie da ein Haufen gezogen kommt und dort ein andrer, wie sie über einen Hügel kamen und bei einer Mühle hielten, wie viel da geblieben sind, wie viel dort, und wie sie sich drängen, und einer gewinnt, der andre verliert, ohne daß man sein Tage begreift, wer was gewinnt oder verliert. Wie eine Stadt eingenommen wird, die Bürger ermordet werden, und wie's den armen Weibern, den unschuldigen Kindern ergeht. Das ist eine Noth und Angst,[57] man denkt jeden Augenblick: Da kommen sie! Es geht uns auch so.

Soest. Drum muß auch ein Bürger immer in Waffen geübt sein.

Jetter. Ja, es übt sich, wer Frau und Kinder hat. Und doch hör' ich noch lieber von Soldaten, als ich sie sehe.

---

[54] Frisch, ihr Herren! Come, quick, gentlemen.

[55] bring' auch deine Gesundheit, let us have your toast.

[56] wie lumpig aber unser einem dabei zu Muthe ist, how miserable we, however, feel.

[57] Das ist eine Noth und Angst, that is a misery and wretchedness.

Buyck. Das sollt' ich übel nehmen.[58]

Jetter. Auf euch ist's nicht gesagt, Landsmann. Wie wir die spanischen Besatzungen los waren, holten wir wieder Athem.

Soest. Gelt![59] die lagen dir am schwersten auf?

Jetter. Vexir' Er sich.

Soest. Die hatten scharfe Einquartierung bei dir.

Jetter. Halt dein Maul.

Soest. Sie hatten ihn vertrieben aus der Küche, dem Keller, der Stube — dem Bette.

(Sie lachen.)

Jetter. Du bist ein Tropf.[60]

Buyck. Friede, ihr Herren! Muß der Soldat Friede rufen? — Nun da ihr von uns nichts hören wollt, nun bringt auch eure Gesundheit aus, eine bürgerliche Gesundheit.

Jetter. Dazu sind wir bereit! Sicherheit und Ruhe!

Soest. Ordnung und Freiheit!

Buyck. Brav! das sind auch wir zufrieden.

(Sie stoßen an und wiederholen fröhlich die Worte, doch so, daß jeder ein anderes ausruft, und es eine Art Canon[61] wird. Der Alte horcht und fällt auch mit ein.)

Alle. Sicherheit und Ruhe! Ordnung und Freiheit!

---

58 übel nehmen, take amiss.
59 Gelt, bet.
60 Tropf, fool.
61 Canon, catch.

Zweite Scene.

Palast der Regentin.

Margarete von Parma in Jagdkleidern. Hofleute. Pagen. Bediente, nachher Machiavell.

Regentin. Ihr stellt das Jagen ab, ich werde heut' nicht reiten.[1] Sagt Machiavellen,[2] er soll zu mir kommen.

(Alle gehen ab.)

Der Gedanke an diese schrecklichen Begebenheiten läßt mir keine Ruhe! Nichts kann mich ergötzen,[3] nichts mich zerstreuen;[4] immer sind diese Bilder,[5] diese Sorgen vor mir. Nun wird der König sagen, dies sein die Folgen meiner Güte, meiner Nachsicht; und doch sagt mir mein Gewissen jeden Augenblick, das Räthlichste, das Beste gethan zu haben. Sollte ich früher mit dem Sturme des Grimmes diese Flammen anfachen und umhertreiben? Ich hoffte, sie zu umstellen,[6] sie in sich selbst zu verschütten.[7] Ja, was ich mir selbst sage, was ich wohl weiß, entschuldigt mich vor mir selbst; aber wie wird es mein Bruder aufnehmen? Denn, ist es zu läugnen? Der Uebermuth der fremden Lehrer hat sich täglich erhöht; sie haben unser Heiligthum gelästert, die stumpfen Sinne des Pöbels zerrüttet und den

---

Second Scene.

[1] Ihr stellt das Jagen ab, ich werde heute nicht reiten, Countermand the hunt, 'I will not ride to-day.' Margaret of Parma was especially famous for her skill in riding. In this as well as some other accomplishments, in her personal appearance, moustache, and the gout (to attacks of which she was occasionally subject), she appears to have belonged to the sterner sex.

[2] Machiavellen. Not historical. Machiavelli was not a member of the regent's council, which consisted of Berlaymont, Viglius, Arras, Orange, and Egmont; nor does he appear to have been a mere visitor.

[3] mich ergötzen, divert me.

[4] zerstreuen, distract.

[5] Bilder, images.

[6] umstellen, confine.

[7] sie in sich selbst verschütten, to quench them.

Schwindelgeist unter sie gebannt.[8] Unreine Geister haben sich unter die Aufrührer gemischt, und schreckliche Thaten sind geschehen, die zu denken schauderhaft ist, und die ich nun einzeln nach Hofe zu berichten habe,[9] schnell und einzeln, damit mir der allgemeine Ruf nicht zuvor komme, damit der König nicht denke, man wolle noch mehr verheimlichen. Ich sehe kein Mittel, weder strenges, noch gelindes, dem Uebel zu steuern.[10] O, was sind wir Großen auf der Woge der Menschheit? Wir glauben sie zu beherrschen, und sie treibt uns auf und nieder, hin und her.

Regentin. Sind die Briefe an den König aufgesetzt?

Machiavell. In einer Stunde werdet ihr sie unterschreiben können.

Regentin. Habt ihr den Bericht ausführlich genug gemacht?

Machiavell. Ausführlich und umständlich,[11] wie es der König liebt. Ich erzähle, wie zuerst zu St. Omer die bilderstürmerische Wuth[12] sich zeigt. Wie eine rasende Menge, mit

---

[8] den Schwindelgeist unter sie gebannt, introduced a revolutionary spirit.

[9] die ich nun einzeln nach Hofe zu berichten habe, which I now have to report to the king in detail.

[10] dem Uebel zu steuern, to counteract the evil.

[11] ausführlich und umständlich, explicitly and circumstantially.

[12] die bilderstürmerische Wuth, the frenzy of the Iconoclasts. The bands of the Iconoclasts were of the lowest order, and the movement was a sudden explosion of popular revenge against the symbols of a church by which the Reformers had been enduring terrible persecution. Roman Catholic writers assert that it was promoted by the wealthier Protestants, while, on the other hand, many believed that the Catholics themselves had planned this outrage in the beginning, in order to bring odium upon the Protestants. Both statements are equally wide of the mark. It is difficult now to say where the movement began, and how it ended, as but few days sufficed to complete the demoniacal work of destruction. The number of churches destroyed is almost incredible. In Flanders alone four hundred were sacked. Singing the verses of Marot's version of the Ten Commandments—

> Taillier ne te feras image
> De quelque chose que ce soit,
> Sy honneur luy fais ou hommage,
> Bon Dieu jalousie en reçoit—

they burst into the churches, and swept away all the vestiges of decorative art, unchecked by the more sober inhabitants. It is worthy of notice that the movement was exclusively directed against the images and statuary,

Stäben, Beilen, Hämmern, Leitern, Stricken versehen, von wenig Bewaffneten begleitet, erst Kapellen, Kirchen und Klöster anfallen, die Andächtigen verjagen, die verschlossenen Pforten aufbrechen, alles umkehren,[13] die Altäre niederreißen, die Statuen der Heiligen zerschlagen, alle Gemälde verderben, alles, was sie nur Geweihtes, Geheiligtes[14] antreffen, zerschmettern, zerreißen zertreten. Wie sich der Hause unterwegs vermehrt, die Einwohner von Ypern ihnen die Thore eröffnen. Wie sie den Dom mit unglaublicher Schnelle verwüsten, die Bibliothek des Bischofs verbrennen. Wie eine große Menge Volks, von gleichem Unsinn ergriffen, sich über Menin, Comines, Verwich,[15] Lille verbreitet, nirgend Widerstand findet, und wie fast durch ganz Flandern in Einem Augenblicke die ungeheure Verschwörung sich erklärt und ausgeführt ist.

Regentin. Ach, wie ergreift mich aufs neue der Schmerz bei deiner Wiederholung! Und die Furcht gesellt sich dazu,[16] das Uebel werde nur größer und größer werden. Sagt mir eure Gedanken, Machiavell!

Machiavell. Verzeihen Eure Hoheit, meine Gedanken sehen Grillen so ähnlich;[17] und wenn ihr auch immer mit meinen Diensten zufrieden wart, habt ihr doch selten meinem Rath folgen mögen. Ihr sagtet oft im Scherze: Du siehst zu weit, Machiavell! Du solltest Geschichtschreiber sein: wer handelt, muß fürs Nächste sorgen. Und doch, habe ich diese Geschichte nicht voraus erzählt? Hab' ich nicht alles voraus gesehen?

Regentin. Ich sehe auch viel voraus, ohne es ändern zu können.

Machiavell. Ein Wort für tausend: Ihr unterdrückt die

---

and that not a man was wounded, nor a woman outraged, that, indeed, prisoners who had for years languished in dungeons were set at liberty.

[13] alles umkehren, overturn everything.

[14] Geweihtes, Geheiligtes, consecrated, hallowed.

[15] Verwich, Verviers.

[16] gesellt sich dazu, accompanies it; das Uebel werde, lest the evil become.

[17] sehen Grillen so ähnlich, are so like whims.

neue Lehre nicht. Laßt sie gelten,[18] sondert sie von den Rechtgläubigen, gebt ihnen Kirchen, faßt sie in die bürgerliche Ordnung, schränkt sie ein; und so habt ihr die Aufrührer auf einmal zur Ruhe gebracht. Jede andern Mittel sind vergeblich, und ihr verheert das Land.

Regentin. Hast du vergessen, mit welchem Abscheu mein Bruder selbst die Frage verwarf, ob man die neue Lehre dulden könne? Weißt du nicht, wie er mir in jedem Briefe die Erhaltung des wahren Glaubens aufs eifrigste empfiehlt? daß er Ruhe und Einigkeit auf Kosten der Religion nicht hergestellt wissen will? Hält er nicht selbst in den Provinzen Spione,[19] die wir nicht kennen, um zu erfahren, wer sich zu der neuen Meinung hinüber neigt? Hat er nicht zu unsrer Verwunderung uns diesen und jenen genannt, der sich in unsrer Nähe heimlich der Ketzerei schuldig machte? Befiehlt er nicht Strenge und Schärfe? Und ich soll gelind sein? ich soll Vorschläge thun, daß er nachsehe, daß er dulde? Würde ich nicht alles Vertrauen, allen Glauben bei ihm verlieren?[20]

Machiavell. Ich weiß wohl; der König befiehlt, er läßt euch seine Absichten wissen. Ihr sollt Ruhe und Friede wieder herstellen, durch ein Mittel, das die Gemüther noch mehr erbittert, das den Krieg unvermeidlich an allen Enden anblasen wird.[21] Bedenkt, was ihr thut. Die größten Kaufleute sind angesteckt,[22] der Adel, das Volk, die Soldaten. Was hilft es, auf seinen Gedanken beharren, wenn sich um uns alles ändert? Möchte doch ein guter Geist Philippen eingeben, daß es einem Könige anständiger ist, Bürger zweierlei Glaubens zu regieren, als sie durch einander aufzureiben.[23]

Regentin. Solch ein Wort nie wieder! Ich weiß wohl,

---

[18] Laßt sie gelten, Let it stand.

[19] Hält er nicht selbst Spione? Does he not even keep spies?

[20] Würde ich nicht alles Vertrauen, allen Glauben bei ihm verlieren? Should I not lose all his confidence, all his faith?

[21] das den Krieg unvermeidlich an allen Enden anblasen wird, that inevitably will fan the war on all sides.

[22] angesteckt, tainted.

[23] aufzureiben, to destroy.

daß Politik selten Treu' und Glauben[24] halten kann, daß sie Offenheit, Gutherzigkeit, Nachgiebigkeit aus unsern Herzen ausschließt. In weltlichen Geschäften ist das leider nur zu wahr; sollen wir aber auch mit Gott spielen, wie unter einander? Sollen wir gleichgültig gegen unsre bewährte Lehre sein, für die so viele ihr Leben aufgeopfert haben? Die sollten wir hingeben an hergelaufne, ungewisse, sich selbst widersprechende Neuerungen?

Machiavell. Denkt nur deßwegen nicht übler von mir.

Regentin. Ich kenne dich und deine Treue und weiß, daß einer ein ehrlicher und verständiger Mann sein kann, wenn er gleich den nächsten besten Weg zum Heil seiner Seele verfehlt hat.[25] Es sind noch andere, Machiavell, Männer, die ich schätzen und tadeln muß.

Machiavell. Wen bezeichnet ihr mir?

Regentin. Ich kann es gestehen, daß mir Egmont heute einen recht innerlichen, tiefen Verdruß erregte.[26]

Machiavell. Durch welches Betragen?

Regentin. Durch sein gewöhnliches, durch Gleichgültigkeit und Leichtsinn. Ich erhielt die schreckliche Botschaft, eben als ich, von vielen und ihm begleitet, aus der Kirche ging. Ich hielt meinen Schmerz nicht an,[27] ich beklagte mich laut und rief, indem ich mich zu ihm wendete: „Seht, was in eurer Provinz entsteht! Das duldet ihr, Graf, von dem der König sich alles versprach?"

Machiavell. Und was antwortete er?

Regentin. Als wenn es nichts, als wenn es eine Nebensache[28] wäre, versetzte er: Wären nur erst die Niederländer über ihre Verfassung beruhigt! Das übrige würde sich leicht geben.

---

[24] Treu' und Glauben halten kann, can keep faith.

[25] wenn er gleich den nächsten besten Weg zum Heil seiner Seele verfehlt hat, though he may have missed the nearest and best road to the salvation of his soul.

[26] daß mir Egmont heute einen recht innerlichen, tiefen Verdruß erregte, that Egmont caused me today a deep heart-felt annoyance.

[27] hielt meinen Schmerz nicht an, did not contain my grief.

[28] eine Nebensache, a secondary matter.

Machiavell. Vielleicht hat er wahrer, als klug und fromm gesprochen. Wie soll Zutrauen entstehen und bleiben, wenn der Niederländer sieht, daß es mehr um seine Besitzthümer als um sein Wohl, um seiner Seele Heil zu thun ist?[29] Haben die neuen Bischöfe mehr Seelen gerettet, als fette Pfründen geschmaust,[30] und sind es nicht meist Fremde? Noch werden alle Statthalterschaften[31] mit Niederländern besetzt; lassen sich es die Spanier nicht zu deutlich merken, daß sie die größte, unwiderstehlichste Begierde nach diesen Stellen empfinden? Will ein Volk nicht lieber nach seiner Art von den Seinigen regieret werden, als von Fremden, die erst im Lande sich wieder Besitzthümer auf Unkosten aller zu erwerben suchen, die einen fremden Maaßstab[32] mitbringen und unfreundlich und ohne Theilnehmung[33] herrschen?

Regentin. Du stellst dich auf die Seite der Gegner.

Machiavell. Mit dem Herzen gewiß nicht; und wollte, ich könnte mit dem Verstande ganz auf der unsrigen sein.

Regentin. Wenn du so willst, so thät' es noth, ich träte ihnen meine Regentschaft ab;[34] denn Egmont und Oranien[35] machten sich große Hoffnung, diesen Platz einzunehmen. Damals waren sie Gegner; jetzt sind sie gegen mich verbunden, sind Freunde, unzertrennliche Freunde geworden.

Machiavell. Ein gefährliches Paar.

Regentin. Soll ich aufrichtig reden; ich fürchte Oranien und ich fürchte für Egmont. Oranien sinnt nichts Gutes, seine Gedanken reichen in die Ferne, er ist heimlich, scheint alles anzunehmen, widerspricht nie, und in tiefster Ehrfurcht, mit größter Vorsicht thut er, was ihm beliebt.

Machiavell. Recht im Gegentheil geht Egmont einen freien Schritt, als wenn die Welt ihm gehörte.

---

[29] mehr zu thun ist um, more a question of.

[30] als fette Pfründen geschmaust, than eaten up fat prebends.

[31] Statthalterschaften, vice-royalties.

[32] Maaßstab, rule, lit. measure.

[33] Theilnehmung, sympathy.

[34] ich träte ihnen meine Regentschaft ab, I gave up to them my regency.

[35] Oranien. *Vide* Introduction.

Regentin. Er trägt das Haupt so hoch, als wenn die Hand der Majestät nicht über ihm schwebte.

Machiavell. Die Augen des Volks sind alle nach ihm gerichtet, und die Herzen hängen an ihm.

Regentin. Nie hat er einen Schein vermieden; als wenn niemand Rechenschaft von ihm zu fordern[36] hätte. Noch trägt er den Namen Egmont. Graf Egmont freut ihn sich nennen zu hören; als wollte er nicht vergessen, daß seine Vorfahren Besitzer von Geldern waren. Warum nennt er sich nicht Prinz von Gaure,[37] wie es ihm zukommt? Warum thut er das? Will er erloschne Rechte wieder geltend machen?[38]

Machiavell. Ich halte ihn für einen treuen Diener des Königs.

Regentin. Wenn er wollte, wie verdient könnte er sich um die Regierung machen;[39] anstatt daß er uns schon, ohne sich zu nutzen, unsäglichen Verdruß gemacht hat. Seine Gesellschaften, Gastmahle und Gelage haben den Adel mehr verbunden und verknüpft, als die gefährlichsten heimlichen Zusammenkünfte. Mit seinen Gesundheiten haben die Gäste einen dauernden Rausch, einen nie sich verziehenden Schwindel[40] geschöpft. Wie oft setzt er durch seine Scherzreden die Gemüther des Volks in Bewegung, und wie stutzte der Pöbel über die neuen Livreen, über die thörichten Abzeichen der Bedienten!

Machiavell. Ich bin überzeugt, es war ohne Absicht.

Regentin. Schlimm genug. Wie ich sage: er schadet uns und nützt sich nicht. Er nimmt das Ernstliche scherzhaft, und wir, um nicht müßig und nachlässig zu scheinen, müssen das Scherzhafte ernstlich nehmen. So hetzt eins das andre;[41] und

---

[36] Rechenschaft fordern, to call to account.

[37] Prinz von Gaure. The count inherited the title from his mother, Frances of Luxemburg, Princess of Gavere, or Gaure.

[38] Will er verloschne Rechte wieder geltend machen? Will he revive obsolete claims?

[39] verdient machen, to render services.

[40] nie sich verziehenden Schwindel, never abating giddiness.

[41] So hetzt eins das andre, One thing engenders, lit. drives, the other.

was man abzuwenden sucht, das macht sich erst recht.[42] Er ist gefährlicher als ein entschiednes Haupt einer Verschwörung; und ich müßte mich sehr irren, wenn man ihm bei Hofe nicht alles gedenkt.[43] Ich kann nicht läugnen, es vergeht wenig Zeit, daß er mich nicht empfindlich, sehr empfindlich macht.

Machiavell. Er scheint mir in allem nach seinem Gewissen zu handeln.

Regentin. Sein Gewissen hat einen gefälligen Spiegel.[44] Sein Betragen ist oft beleidigend. Er sieht oft aus, als wenn er in der völligen Ueberzeugung lebe, er sei Herr, und wolle es uns nur aus Gefälligkeit nicht fühlen lassen, wolle uns so gerade nicht zum Lande hinausjagen; es werde sich schon geben.[45]

Machiavell. Ich bitte euch, legt seine Offenheit, sein glückliches Blut, das alles Wichtige leicht behandelt, nicht zu gefährlich aus.[46] Ihr schadet nur ihm und euch.

Regentin. Ich lege nichts aus. Ich spreche nur von den unvermeidlichen Folgen, und ich kenne ihn. Sein niederländischer Adel und sein golden Vließ vor der Brust stärken sein Vertrauen, seine Kühnheit. Beides kann ihn vor einem schnellen, willkürlichen Unmuth des Königs schützen.[47] Untersuch' es genau; an dem ganzen Unglück, das Flandern trifft, ist er doch nur allein schuld. Er hat zuerst den fremden Lehrern nachgesehn,[48] hat's so genau nicht genommen und vielleicht sich heimlich gefreut, daß wir etwas zu schaffen hatten.[49] Laß mich nur.

---

[42] macht sich erst recht, is sure to happen.

[43] einem etwas gedenken, to reckon up, to lay to one's charge.

[44] gefälligen Spiegel, convenient reflection, lit. mirror.

[45] es werde sich schon geben, matters would alter.

[46] legt seine Offenheit . . . nicht zu gefährlich aus, do not interpret his frankness as too dangerous.

[47] Beides kann ihn . . . schützen, Both things may save him [from a sudden arbitrary anger of the king]. The knights of the Golden Fleece enjoyed special immunities and privileges. They could only be judged in full chapter, of which the sovereign, as lord paramount and head of the order, was the president, and had only the casting vote.

[48] hat den fremden Lehrern nachgesehn, has been indulgent to the foreign teachers; hat's so genau nicht genommen, has not been very strict.

[49] daß wir etwas zu schaffen hatten, that we had our troubles.

Was ich auf dem Herzen habe, soll bei dieser Gelegenheit davon.[50] Und ich will die Pfeile nicht umsonst verschießen; ich weiß, wo er empfindlich[51] ist. Er ist auch empfindlich.

Machiavell. Habt ihr den Rath[52] zusammen berufen lassen? Kommt Oranien auch?

Regentin. Ich habe nach Antwerpen um ihn geschickt. Ich will ihnen die Last der Verantwortung[53] nahe genug zuwälzen; sie sollen sich mit mir dem Uebel ernstlich entgegensetzen oder sich auch als Rebellen erklären. Eile, daß die Briefe fertig werden, und bringe mir sie zur Unterschrift. Dann sende schnell den bewährten Vaska[54] nach Madrid; er ist unermüdet und treu; daß mein Bruder zuerst durch ihn die Nachricht erfahre, daß der Ruf ihn nicht übereile.[55] Ich will ihn selbst noch sprechen, eh' er abgeht.

Machiavell. Eure Befehle sollen schnell und genau befolgt werden.

Dritte Scene.

Bürgerhaus.

Clare. Clarens Mutter. Brackenburg.

Clare. Wollt ihr mir nicht das Garn halten, Brackenburg?

Brackenburg. Ich bitt' euch, verschont mich,[1] Clärchen.

Clare. Was habt ihr wieder? Warum versagt ihr mir diesen kleinen Liebesdienst?

Brackenburg. Ihr bannt mich mit dem Zwirn so fest vor euch hin,[2] ich kann euern Augen nicht ausweichen.

---

[50] soll davon, shall have vent.
[51] empfindlich, vulnerable.
[52] Rath, council.
[53] Verantwortung, responsibility.
[54] Vaska. Not historical.
[55] ihn nicht übereile, may not precede him.

Third Scene.

[1] verschont mich, spare me.
[2] Ihr bannt mich mit dem Zwirn so fest vor euch hin, You hold me enchanted [in the folds of], lit. with the yarn.

Clare. Grillen! kommt und haltet!

Mutter (im Sessel strickend). Singt doch eins! Brackenburg secundirt so hübsch.[3] Sonst wart ihr lustig, und ich hatte immer was zu lachen.

Brackenburg. Sonst.

Clare. Wir wollen singen.

Brackenburg. Was ihr wollt.

Clare. Nur hübsch munter und frisch weg![4] Es ist ein Soldatenliedchen, mein Leibstück.[5]

(Sie wickelt Garn und singt mit Brackenburg.)

Die Trommel gerühret![6]
Das Pfeifchen gespielt!
Mein Liebster gewaffnet
Dem Haufen befiehlt,
Die Lanze hoch führet,
Die Leute regieret.
Wie klopft mir das Herze!
Wie wallt mir das Blut![7]
O, hätt' ich ein Wämmslein,[8]
Und Hosen und Hut!

Ich folgt'[9] ihm zum Thor 'naus
Mit muthigem Schritt,
Ging' durch die Provinzen,
Ging' überall mit.
Die Feinde schon weichen,
Wir schießen dadrein.[10]
Welch Glück sonder Gleichen,
Ein Mannsbild[11] zu sein!

---

[3] secundirt so hübsch, sings such a pretty second.

[4] Nur hübsch munter und frisch weg! Sing away merrily and lustily.

[5] mein Leibstück, my favourite.

[6] gerühret, beaten. The past part. stands here for imper. mood.

[7] Wie wallt mir das Blut! How swiftly courses my blood.

[8] Wämmslein, coat.

[9] folgte, ginge; conditional. I should follow, go.

[10] Wir schießen dadrein, we fire amongst them.

[11] Mannsbild, compound substantive for Mann. Comp. Frauenbild.

(Brackenburg hat unter dem Singen Clärchen oft angesehen; zuletzt bleibt ihm die Stimme stocken, die Thränen kommen ihm in die Augen, er läßt den Strang fallen und geht ans Fenster. Clärchen singt das Lied allein aus, die Mutter winkt ihr halb unwillig, sie steht auf, geht einige Schritte nach ihm hin, kehrt halb unschlüssig[12] wieder um und setzt sich.)

Mutter. Was giebt's auf der Gasse, Brackenburg? Ich höre marschiren.

Brackenburg. Es ist die Leibwache[13] der Regentin.

Clare. Um diese Stunde? was soll das bedeuten? (Sie steht auf und geht an das Fenster zu Brackenburg). Das ist nicht die tägliche Wache, das sind weit mehr! Fast alle ihre Haufen. O, Brackenburg, geht! hört einmal, was es giebt? Es muß etwas Besonderes sein. Geht, guter Brackenburg, thut mir den Gefallen.

Brackenburg. Ich gehe! Ich bin gleich wieder da. (Er reicht ihr abgehend die Hand; sie giebt ihm die ihrige.)

Mutter. Du schickst ihn schon wieder weg.

Clare. Ich bin neugierig; und auch, verdenkt mir's nicht,[14] seine Gegenwart thut mir weh. Ich weiß immer nicht, wie ich mich gegen ihn betragen soll. Ich habe Unrecht gegen ihn, und mich nagt's am Herzen,[15] daß er es so lebendig fühlt. — Kann ich's doch nicht ändern!

Mutter. Es ist ein so treuer Bursche.

Clare. Ich kann's auch nicht lassen, ich muß ihm freundlich begegnen. Meine Hand drückt sich oft unversehens zu,[16] wenn die seine mich so leise, so liebevoll anfaßt. Ich mache mir Vorwürfe, daß ich ihn betrüge, daß ich in seinem Herzen eine vergebliche Hoffnung nähre. Ich bin übel dran.[17] Weiß Gott, ich betrüg' ihn nicht. Ich will nicht, daß er hoffen soll, und ich kann ihn doch nicht verzweifeln lassen.

---

[12] halb unschlüssig, half irresolute.

[13] Leibwache, body-guard.

[14] verdenkt mir's nicht, do not find fault with me for it.

[15] mich nagt's am Herzen, my heart is grieved.

[16] Meine Hand drückt sich oft unversehens zu, my hand often unintentionally presses his.

[17] bin übel dran, am in a strait.

Mutter. Das ist nicht gut.

Clare. Ich hatte ihn gern und will ihm auch noch wohl in der Seele.[18] Ich hätte ihn heirathen können und glaube, ich war nie in ihn verliebt.

Mutter. Glücklich wärst du immer mit ihm gewesen.

Clare. Wäre versorgt[19] und hätte ein ruhiges Leben.

Mutter. Und das ist alles durch deine Schuld verscherzt.[20]

Clare. Ich bin in einer wunderlichen Lage. Wenn ich so nachdenke, wie es gegangen ist, weiß ich's wohl und weiß es nicht. Und dann darf ich Egmont nur wieder ansehen, wird mir alles sehr begreiflich,[21] ja wäre mir weit mehr begreiflich. Ach, was ist's ein Mann! Alle Provinzen beten ihn an, und ich in seinem Arm sollte nicht das glücklichste Geschöpf von der Welt sein?

Mutter. Wie wird's in der Zukunft werden?

Clare. Ach, ich frage nur, ob er mich liebt; und ob er mich liebt, ist das eine Frage?

Mutter. Man hat nichts als Herzensangst[22] mit seinen Kindern. Wie das ausgehen wird! Immer Sorge und Kummer! Es geht nicht gut aus![23] Du hast dich unglücklich gemacht! mich unglücklich gemacht!

Clare (gelassen). Ihr ließet es doch[24] im Anfange.

Mutter. Leider war ich zu gut, bin immer zu gut.

Clare. Wenn Egmont vorbeiritt und ich ans Fenster lief, schaltet ihr mich da? Tratet ihr nicht selbst ans Fenster? Wenn er herauf sah, lächelte, nickte, mich grüßte, war es euch zuwider?[25] Fandet ihr euch nicht selbst in eurer Tochter geehrt?

Mutter. Mache mir noch Vorwürfe.[26]

Clare (gerührt). Wenn er nun öfter die Straße kam, und

---

[18] will ich ihm noch wohl in der Seele, like him in my heart still.

[19] wäre versorgt, should have been provided for.

[20] das ist alles durch deine Schuld verscherzt, all that has been trifled away by your own folly.

[21] mir wird alles sehr begreiflich, everything becomes plain to me.

[22] nichts als seine Herzensangst, nothing but care.

[23] ausgehen, terminate.

[24] Ihr ließet es doch, yet you permitted it.

[25] war es euch zuwider? was it against your wish?

[26] Mache mir noch Vorwürfe, Reproach me into the bargain.

wir wohl fühlten, daß er um meinetwillen den Weg machte, bemerktet ihr's nicht selbst mit heimlicher Freude? Rieft ihr mich ab, wenn ich hinter den Scheiben stand[27] und ihn erwartete?

Mutter. Dachte ich, daß es so weit kommen sollte?

Clare (mit stockender Stimme und zurückgehaltenen Thränen). Und wie er uns Abends, in den Mantel eingehüllt, bei der Lampe überraschte, wer war geschäftig, ihn zu empfangen, da ich auf meinem Stuhl wie angekettet[28] und staunend sitzen blieb?

Mutter. Und konnte ich fürchten, daß diese unglückliche Liebe das kluge Clärchen so bald hinreißen würde? Ich muß es nun tragen, daß meine Tochter —

Clare (mit ausbrechenden Thränen). Mutter! Ihr wollt's nun! Ihr habt eure Freude, mich zu ängstigen.

Mutter (weinend). Weine noch gar![29] mache mich noch elender durch deine Betrübniß! Ist mir's nicht Kummer genug, daß meine einzige Tochter ein verworfenes Geschöpf ist?

Clare (aufstehend und kalt). Verworfen! Egmonts Geliebte, verworfen? — Welche Fürstin neidete nicht das arme Clärchen um den Platz an seinem Herzen! O, Mutter — meine Mutter, so redetet ihr sonst nicht. Liebe Mutter, seid gut! Das Volk, was das denkt, die Nachbarinnen, was die murmeln — Diese Stube, dieses kleine Haus ist ein Himmel, seit Egmonts Liebe drin wohnt.

Mutter. Man muß ihm hold sein! das ist wahr. Er ist wahr. Er ist immer so freundlich, frei und offen.

Clare. Es ist keine falsche Ader an ihm.[30] Seht, Mutter, und er ist doch der große Egmont. Und wenn er zu mir kommt, wie er so lieb ist, so gut! wie er mir seinen Stand, seine Tapferkeit gerne verbärge! wie er um mich besorgt ist! so nur Mensch, nur Freund, nur Liebster.

Mutter. Kommt er wohl heute?

---

[27] wenn ich hinter den Scheiben stand, when I stood at the window.

[28] wie angekettet, as if I had been chained.

[29] noch gar, into the bargain.

[30] Es ist keine falsche Ader an ihm, There is nothing false (lit. no false vein) in him.

Clare. Habt ihr mich nicht oft ans Fenster gehen sehn? Habt ihr nicht bemerkt, wie ich horche, wenn's an der Thüre rauscht? — Ob ich schon weiß,[31] daß er vor Nacht nicht kommt, vermuth' ich ihn doch jeden Augenblick, von Morgens an, wenn ich aufstehe. Wär' ich nur ein Bube und könnte immer mit ihm gehen, zu Hofe und überall hin! Könnt' ihm die Fahne nachtragen in der Schlacht! —

Mutter. Du warst immer so ein Springinsfeld;[32] als ein kleines Kind schon, bald toll, bald nachdenklich. Ziehst du dich nicht ein wenig besser an?[33]

Clare. Vielleicht, Mutter! wenn ich Langeweile habe. — Gestern, denkt, gingen von seinen Leuten vorbei und sangen Lobliedchen auf ihn. Wenigstens war sein Name in den Liedern; das übrige konnt' ich nicht verstehn. Das Herz schlug mir bis an den Hals.[34] — Ich hätte sie gern zurückgerufen, wenn ich mich nicht geschämt hätte.

Mutter. Nimm dich in Acht! Dein heftiges Wesen verdirbt noch alles; du verräthst dich offenbar vor den Leuten. Wie neulich bei dem Vetter, wie du den Holzschnitt und die Beschreibung[35] fandst und mit einem Schrei riefst: Graf Egmont! — Ich ward feuerroth.

Clare. Hätt' ich nicht schreien sollen? Es war die Schlacht bei Gravelingen; und ich finde oben im Bilde den Buchstaben C. und suche unten in der Beschreibung C. Steht da: „Graf Egmont, dem das Pferd unter dem Leibe todt geschossen wird." Mich überlief's[36] — und hernach mußt' ich lachen über den holzgeschnitzten Egmont, der so groß war als der Thurm von Gravelingen gleich dabei und die englischen Schiffe an der Seite. — Wenn ich mich manchmal erinnere, wie ich mir sonst eine Schlacht

---

[31] Ob ich schon weiß, i.q. obschon ich weiß.

[32] Springinsfeld, hoiden.

[33] Ziehst du dich nicht ein wenig besser an? Will you not put on a better dress?

[34] Das Herz schlug mir bis an den Hals, My heart leaped up into my throat.

[35] den Holzschnitt und die Beschreibung, the woodcut with the description.

[36] Mich überlief's, a cold shudder ran over me.

vorgestellt, und was ich mir als Mädchen für ein Bild vom Grafen Egmont machte, wenn sie von ihm erzählten, und von allen Grafen und Fürsten — und wie mir's jetzt ist![37]

Brackenburg kommt.

Clare. Wie steht's?

Brackenburg. Man weiß nichts Gewisses. In Flandern soll neuerdings ein Tumult entstanden sein;[38] die Regentin soll besorgen, er möchte sich hierher verbreiten.[39] Das Schloß ist stark besetzt, die Bürger sind zahlreich an den Thoren, das Volk summt[40] in den Gassen. — Ich will nur schnell zu meinem alten Vater.

(Als wollte er gehen.)

Clare. Sieht man euch morgen? Ich will mich ein wenig anziehen. Der Vetter kommt, und ich sehe gar zu liederlich[41] aus. Helft mir einen Augenblick, Mutter. — Nehmt das Buch mit, Brackenburg, und bringt mir wieder so eine Historie.

Mutter. Lebt wohl.

Brackenburg (seine Hand reichend). Eure Hand!

Clare (ihre Hand versagend). Wenn ihr wieder kommt.

(Mutter und Tochter ab).

Brackenburg (allein). Ich hatte mir vorgenommen, grade wieder fort zu gehn; und da sie es dafür aufnimmt[42] und mich gehen läßt, möcht' ich rasend werden. — Unglücklicher! und dich rührt deines Vaterlandes Geschick nicht? der wachsende Tumult nicht? — und gleich ist dir[43] Landsmann oder Spanier, und wer regiert und wer Recht hat? — War ich doch ein andrer Junge als Schulknabe! — Wenn da ein Exercitium aufgegeben war: „Brutus Rede für die Freiheit, zur Uebung der Redekunst;“ da

---

37 wie mir's jetzt ist, how I feel now.

38 soll entstanden sein, is said to have broken out.

39 verbreiten, spread.

40 summt, lit. hums, is talking.

41 liederlich, slovenly.

42 da sie es dafür aufnimmt, since she believes it; i. q. da sie es als Ernst aufnimmt, since she takes it seriously.

43 gleich ist dir, it is the same to you.

war doch immer Fritz der Erste, und der Rector sagte: wenn's nur ordentlicher wäre, nur nicht alles so über einander gestolpert.[44] — Damals kocht' es und trieb es![45] — Jetzt schlepp' ich mich an den Augen des Mädchens so hin. Kann ich sie doch nicht lassen! Kann sie mich doch nicht lieben! — Ach — Nein — Sie — Sie kann mich nicht ganz verworfen haben[46] — — Nicht ganz — und halb und nichts! — Ich duld' es nicht länger! — — Sollte es wahr sein, was mir ein Freund neulich ins Ohr sagte? daß sie Nachts einen Mann heimlich zu sich einläßt, da sie mich züchtig immer vor Abend aus dem Hause treibt. Nein, es ist nicht wahr, es ist eine Lüge, eine schändliche verleumderische Lüge! Clärchen ist so unschuldig, als ich unglücklich bin. — Sie hat mich verworfen, hat mich von ihrem Herzen gestoßen. — — Und ich soll so fort leben? Ich duld', ich duld' es nicht. — — Schon wird mein Vaterland von innerm Zwiste[47] heftiger bewegt, und ich sterbe unter dem Getümmel nur ab! Ich duld' es nicht! — Wenn die Trompete klingt, ein Schuß fällt, mir fährt's durch Mark und Bein![48] Ach, es reizt mich nicht! es fordert mich nicht, auch mit einzugreifen, mit zu retten, zu wagen. — Elender, schimpflicher Zustand! Es ist besser, ich end' auf einmal. Neulich stürzt' ich mich ins Wasser, ich sank — aber die geängstete Natur war stärker; ich fühlte, daß ich schwimmen konnte, und rettete mich wider Willen. — — Könnt' ich der Zeiten vergessen, da sie mich liebte, mich zu lieben schien! — Warum hat mir's Mark und Bein durchdrungen, das Glück? Warum haben mir diese Hoffnungen allen Genuß des Lebens aufgezehrt,[49] indem sie mir ein Paradies von weitem zeigten? — Und jener erste Kuß! Jener einzige! — Hier (die Hand auf den

---

[44] wenn's nur nicht alles so über einander gestolpert wäre, if you only did not blunder it out so quickly.

[45] Damals kocht' es und trieb es! At that time, I was all fire and flames.

[46] Sie kann mich nicht ganz verworfen haben, She cannot have rejected me altogether.

[47] von innerm Zwiste, with internal dissension.

[48] mir fährt's durch Mark und Bein, it goes through me.

[49] Warum haben mir diese Hoffnungen allen Genuß des Lebens aufgezehrt? Why have these hopes eaten up all life's enjoyments?

Tisch legend), hier waren wir allein — sie war immer gut und freundlich gegen mich gewesen — da schien sie sich zu erweichen — sie sah mich an — alle Sinne gingen mir um,[50] und ich fühlte ihre Lippen auf den meinigen. — Und — und nun? — Stirb, Armer! Was zauderst du? (Er zieht ein Fläschchen aus der Tasche.) Ich will dich nicht umsonst aus meines Bruders Doctorkästchen[51] gestohlen haben, heilsames Gift! Du sollst mir dieses Bangen, diese Schwindel, diese Todesschweiße auf einmal verschlingen und lösen.[52]

---

[50] alle Sinne gingen mir um, all my senses were in a whirl.

[51] Doctorkästchen, medicine-chest.

[52] lösen, lit. to loosen, to set free; here to set free from, to cure.

Zweiter Aufzug.

Erste Szene.

Platz in Brüssel.

Jetter und ein Zimmermeister treten zusammen.

Zimmermeister. Sagt' ich's nicht voraus? Noch vor acht Tagen auf der Zunft[1] sagt' ich, es würde schwere Händel geben.[2]

Jetter. Ist's denn wahr, daß sie die Kirchen in Flandern geplündert haben?

Zimmermeister. Ganz und gar zu Grunde gerichtet[3] haben sie Kirchen und Kapellen. Nichts als die vier nackten Wände haben sie stehen lassen. Lauter Lumpengesindel![4] Und das macht unsre gute Sache schlimm. Wir hätten eher, in der Ordnung und standhaft, unsere Gerechtsame[5] der Regentin vortragen und drauf halten sollen. Reden wir jetzt, versammeln wir uns jetzt, so heißt es, wir gesellen uns zu den Aufwieglern.

Jetter. Ja, so denkt jeder zuerst: was sollst du mit deiner Nase voran?[6] hängt doch der Hals gar nah' damit zusammen.

Zimmermeister. Mir ist's bange, wenn's einmal unter dem Pack zu lärmen anfängt, unter dem Volk, das nichts zu verlieren hat. Die brauchen das zum Vorwande, worauf wir uns auch berufen müssen,[7] und bringen das Land in Unglück.

---

[1] Zunft, guild; here their hall.

[2] es würde schwere Händel geben, that we should have some serious disturbances.

[3] Ganz und gar zu Grunde gerichtet haben sie, They have totally destroyed.

[4] Lauter Lumpengesindel! A mere rabble!

[5] Gerechtsame, privileges.

[6] was sollst du mit deiner Nase voran? why should you put your nose into it?

[7] Die brauchen das zum Vorwande, worauf wir uns auch berufen müssen, They use as a pretext that with which we have to justify ourselves.

Soest tritt dazu.

Guten Tag, ihr Herren! Was giebt's neues? Ist's wahr, daß die Bilderstürmer gerade hierher ihren Lauf nehmen?

Zimmermeister. Hier sollen sie nichts anrühren.

Soest. Es trat ein Soldat bei mir ein, Tabak zu kaufen; den fragt' ich aus. Die Regentin, so eine wackre kluge Frau sie bleibt, diesmal ist sie außer Fassung.[8] Es muß sehr arg sein, daß sie sich so geradezu hinter ihre Wache versteckt. Die Burg ist scharf besetzt.[9] Man meint sogar, sie wolle aus der Stadt flüchten.

Zimmermeister. Hinaus soll sie nicht! Ihre Gegenwart beschützt uns, und wir wollen ihr mehr Sicherheit verschaffen, als ihre Stutzbärte.[10] Und wenn sie uns unsre Rechte und Freiheiten aufrecht erhält, so wollen wir sie auf den Händen tragen.

Seifensieder tritt dazu.

Garstige Händel! Ueble Händel! Es wird unruhig und geht schief aus![11] — Hütet euch, daß ihr stille bleibt, daß man euch nicht auch für Aufwiegler hält.

Soest. Da kommen die sieben Weisen aus Griechenland.

Seifensieder. Ich weiß, da sind viele, die es heimlich mit den Calvinisten halten, die auf die Bischöfe lästern,[12] die den König nicht scheuen. Aber ein treuer Unterthan, ein aufrichtiger Katholike! —

(Es gesellt sich nach und nach allerlei Volk zu ihnen und horcht.)

Vansen tritt dazu.

Gott grüß' euch Herren! Was neues?

Zimmermeister. Gebt euch mit dem nicht ab,[13] das ist ein schlechter Kerl.

Jetter. Ist es nicht der Schreiber beim Doctor Wiets?

---

[8] diesmal ist sie außer Fassung, this time she is at her wits' end.

[9] Die Burg ist scharf besetzt, The castle is strongly manned.

[10] als ihre Stutzbärte, than her peaked beards; i. e. her Spanish troops.

[11] geht schief aus, will end badly, lit. crookedly.

[12] die auf die Bischöfe lästern, who revile the bishops.

[13] Gebt euch mit dem nicht ab, Have nothing to say to that fellow.

Zimmermeister. Er hat schon viele Herren gehabt. Erst war er Schreiber, und wie ihn ein Patron nach dem andern fortjagte, Schelmstreiche halber, pfuscht er jetzt Notaren und Advocaten ins Handwerk,[14] und ist ein Branntweinzapf.[15]

(Es kommt mehr Volk zusammen und steht truppweise.)

Vansen. Ihr seid auch versammelt, steckt die Köpfe zusammen. Es ist immer redenswerth.

Soest. Ich denk' auch.

Vansen. Wenn jetzt einer oder der andere Herz hätte, und einer oder der andere den Kopf dazu, wir könnten die spanischen Ketten auf einmal sprengen.

Soest. Herre! So müßt ihr nicht reden. Wir haben dem König geschworen.[16]

Vansen. Und der König uns.[17] Merkt das.

Jetter. Das läßt sich hören! Sagt eure Meinung.

Einige Andere. Horch, der versteht's. Der hat Pfiffe.[18]

Vansen. Ich hatte einen alten Patron, der besaß Pergamente und Briefe von uralten Stiftungen,[19] Contracten und Gerechtigkeiten; er hielt auf die rarsten Bücher.[20] In einem stand unsere ganze Verfassung: wie uns Niederländer zuerst einzelne Fürsten regierten, alles nach hergebrachten Rechten, Privilegien und Gewohnheiten; wie unsre Vorfahren alle Ehrfurcht für ihren Fürsten gehabt, wenn er sie regiert, wie er sollte; und wie sie sich gleich vorsahen, wenn er über die Schnur hauen wollte.[21] Die Staaten waren gleich hinterdrein;[22] denn jede Provinz, so klein sie war, hatte ihre Staaten, ihre Landstände.

---

[14] pfuscht er jetzt Notaren und Advocaten ins Handwerk, he dabbles now as a pettifogging lawyer.

[15] Branntweinzapf, swiller of brandy.

[16] dem König geschworen, taken the oath (of allegiance) to the king.

[17] Und der König uns, And the king has taken his (to maintain our privileges).

[18] hat Pfiffe, is clever, deep.

[19] von uralten Stiftungen, of very ancient foundations.

[20] hielt auf die rarsten Bücher, was a lover of rare books.

[21] wie sie sich gleich vorsahen, wenn er über die Schnur hauen wollte, how they immediately took precautionary measures if he attempted any excesses, lit. went beyond his tether.

[22] waren gleich hinterdrein, were after him directly.

Zimmermeister. Haltet euer Maul! das weiß man lange! Ein jeder rechtschaffne Bürger ist, so viel er braucht, von der Verfassung unterrichtet.

Jetter. Laßt ihn reden; man erfährt immer etwas mehr.

Soest. Er hat ganz recht.

Mehrere. Erzählt! erzählt! So was hört man nicht alle Tage.

Vansen. So seid ihr Bürgersleute! Ihr lebt nur so in den Tag hin;[23] und wie ihr euer Gewerb' von euern Eltern überkommen habt, so laßt ihr auch das Regiment über euch schalten und walten, wie es kann und mag. Ihr fragt nicht nach dem Herkommen, nach der Historie, nach dem Recht eines Regenten; und über das Versäumniß[24] haben euch die Spanier das Netz über die Ohren gezogen.

Soest. Wer denkt da dran? wenn einer nur das tägliche Brod hat.

Jetter. Verflucht! Warum tritt auch keiner in Zeiten auf, und sagt einem so etwas?

Vansen. Ich sag' es euch jetzt. Der König in Spanien, der die Provinzen durch gut Glück zusammen besitzt, darf doch nicht drin schalten und walten, anders als die kleinen Fürsten, die sie ehemals einzeln besaßen. Begreift ihr das?

Jetter. Erklärt's uns.

Vansen. Es ist so klar als die Sonne. Müßt ihr nicht nach euern Landrechten gerichtet werden?[25] Woher käme das?

Ein Bürger. Wahrlich!

Vansen. Hat der Brüsseler nicht ein ander Recht als der Antwerper? der Antwerper als der Genter? Woher käme denn das?

Anderer Bürger. Bei Gott!

---

[23] lebt nur so in den Tag hin, live carelessly.

[24] und über das Versäumniß, and while you neglected that.

[25] Müßt ihr nicht nach euern Landrechten gerichtet werden? Have they not to judge you (administer justice) according to the law of the land.

Vansen. Aber, wenn ihr's so fortlaufen laßt,[26] wird man's euch bald anders weisen. Pfui! Was Carl der Kühne, Friedrich der Krieger, Carl der Fünfte nicht konnten, das thut nun Philipp durch ein Weib.

Soest. Ja, ja! die alten Fürsten haben's auch schon probirt.

Vansen. Freilich! — Unsere Vorfahren paßten auf.[27] Wie sie einem Herrn gram wurden,[28] fingen sie ihm etwa seinen Sohn und Erben weg, hielten ihn bei sich, und gaben ihn nur auf die besten Bedingungen heraus. Unsere Väter waren Leute! Die wußten, was ihnen nütz war! Die wußten etwas zu fassen und fest zu setzen! Rechte Männer! Dafür sind aber auch unsere Privilegien so deutlich, unsere Freiheiten so versichert.[29]

Seifensieder. Was sprecht ihr von Freiheiten?

Das Volk. Von unsern Freiheiten, von unsern Privilegien! Erzählt noch was von unsern Privilegien!

Vansen. Wir Brabanter besonders, obgleich alle Provinzen ihre Vortheile haben, wir sind am herrlichsten versehen.[30] Ich habe alles gelesen.

Soest. Sagt an.

Jetter. Laßt hören.

---

[26] Aber, wenn ihr's so fortlaufen laßt, But if you let them go on as they do.

[27] paßten auf, looked after them.

[28] Wie sie einem Herrn gram wurden, When they had a grievance against a lord.

[29] unsere Freiheiten so versichert, our liberties so assured.

[30] Wir Brabanter besonders, . . . wir sind am herrlichsten versehen. The 'Blyde Inkomst,' or *Joyeuse Entrée*, the constitution of Brabant, provided—'That the prince should not elevate the clerical state higher than of old had been customary, and by former princes settled; unless by consent of the other two estates, the nobility and the cities.' 'That the prince should prosecute no one of his subjects, nor any foreign resident, civilly or criminally, except in the ordinary and open courts of justice in the province where the accused might answer and defend himself with the help of advocates.' 'That the prince should appoint no foreigners to office in Brabant;' and, lastly, 'Should the prince by force, or otherwise, violate any of these privileges, the inhabitants of Brabant, after regular protest entered, are discharged of their oaths of allegiance, and, as free, independent, and unbound people, may conduct themselves exactly as seems to them best.'

Ein Bürger. Ich bitt' euch.

Vansen. Erstlich steht geschrieben: Der Herzog von Brabant soll uns ein guter und getreuer Herr sein.

Soest. Gut! Steht das so?

Jetter. Getreu? Ist das wahr?

Vansen. Wie ich euch sage. Er ist uns verpflichtet, wie wir ihm. Zweitens: Er soll keine Macht oder eignen Willen an uns beweisen, merken lassen, oder gedenken zu gestatten,[31] auf keinerlei Weise.

Jetter. Schön! Schön! nicht beweisen.

Soest. Nicht merken lassen.

Ein Anderer. Und nicht gedenken zu gestatten! Das ist der Hauptpunkt. Niemanden gestatten, auf keinerlei Weise.

Vansen. Mit ausdrücklichen Worten.

Jetter. Schafft uns das Buch.

Ein Bürger. Ja, wir müssen's haben.

Andere. Das Buch! das Buch!

Ein Anderer. Wir wollen zu der Regentin gehen mit dem Buche.

Ein Anderer. Ihr sollt das Wort führen,[32] Herr Doctor.

Seifensieder. O, die Tröpfe![33]

Andere. Noch etwas aus dem Buche!

Seifensieder. Ich schlage ihm die Zähne in den Hals, wenn er noch ein Wort sagt.

Das Volk. Wir wollen sehen, wer ihm etwas thut.[34] Sagt uns was von den Privilegien! Haben wir noch mehr Privilegien?

Vansen. Mancherlei, und sehr gute, sehr heilsame. Da steht auch: Der Landsherr soll den geistlichen Stand nicht verbessern oder mehren, ohne Verwilligung des Adels und der Stände! Merkt das! Auch den Staat des Landes nicht verändern.

---

[31] gedenken zu gestatten, intend to permit.

[32] Ihr sollt das Wort führen, You shall be spokesman.

[33] Tröpfe, simpletons, fools. The derivation is uncertain.

[34] Wir wollen sehen, wer ihm etwas thut, We will see who dares to hurt him.

Soest. Ist das so?

Vansen. Ich will's euch geschrieben zeigen, von zwei, dreihundert Jahren her.

Bürger. Und wir leiden die neuen Bischöfe? Der Adel muß uns schützen, wir fangen Händel an!

Andere. Und wir lassen uns von der Inquisition ins Bockshorn jagen?[35]

Vansen. Das ist eure Schuld.

Das Volk. Wir haben noch Egmont! noch Oranien! Die sorgen für unser Bestes.

Vansen. Eure Brüder in Flandern haben das gute Werk angefangen.

Seifensieder. Du Hund!

(Er schlägt ihn.)

Andere (widersetzen sich und rufen). Bist du auch ein Spanier?

Ein Anderer. Was? den Ehrenmann?

Ein Anderer. Den Gelahrten?

(Sie fallen den Seifensieder an.)

Zimmermeister. Um's Himmels willen, ruht! (Andere mischen sich in den Streit.) Bürger, was soll das?

(Buben pfeifen, werfen mit Steinen, hetzen Hunde an,[36] Bürger stehn und gaffen, Volk läuft zu, andere gehn gelassen auf und ab, andere treiben allerlei Schalkspossen, schreien und jubiliren.)

Andere. Freiheit und Privilegien! Privilegien und Freiheit!

Egmont tritt auf mit Begleitung.

Ruhig! Ruhig! Leute! Was giebt's? Ruhe! Bringt sie aus einander![37]

Zimmermeister. Gnädiger Herr, ihr kommt wie ein Engel des Himmels. Stille! seht ihr nichts? Graf Egmont! Dem Grafen Egmont Reverenz!

---

[35] lassen uns von der Inquisition ins Bockshorn jagen, allow ourselves to be frightened by the bugbear of an Inquisition.

[36] hetzen Hunde an, set their dogs on.

[37] Bringt sie aus einander! Separate them.

Egmont. Auch hier? Was fangt ihr an? Bürger gegen Bürger! Hält sogar die Nähe unsrer königlichen Regentin diesen Unsinn nicht zurück?[38] Geht aus einander, geht an euer Gewerbe. Es ist ein übles Zeichen, wenn ihr an Werktagen feiert. Was war's?

(Der Tumult stillt sich nach und nach, und alle stehen um ihn herum.)

Zimmermeister. Sie schlagen sich um ihre Privilegien.

Egmont. Die sie noch muthwillig zertrümmern werden[39] — Und wer seid ihr? Ihr scheint mir rechtliche Leute.

Zimmermeister. Das ist unser Bestreben.[40]

Egmont. Eures Zeichens?[41]

Zimmermeister. Zimmermann und Zunftmeister.

Egmont. Und ihr?

Soest. Krämer.

Egmont. Ihr?

Jetter. Schneider.

Egmont. Ich erinnere mich, ihr habt mit an den Livreen für meine Leute gearbeitet. Euer Name ist Jetter.

Jetter. Gnade, daß[42] ihr euch dessen erinnert.

Egmont. Ich vergesse niemanden leicht, den ich einmal gesehen und gesprochen habe. — Was an euch ist, Ruhe zu erhalten, Leute, das thut; ihr seid übel genug angeschrieben.[43] Reizt den König nicht mehr, er hat zuletzt doch die Gewalt in Händen. Ein ordentlicher Bürger, der sich ehrlich und fleißig nährt, hat überall so viel Freiheit, als er braucht.

Zimmermeister. Ach wohl! das ist eben unsre Noth! Die Tagdiebe, die Söffer, die Faulenzer, mit Euer Gnaden Verlaub, die stänkern[44] aus Langerweile, und scharren aus Hunger

---

38 Hält sogar die Nähe unserer königlichen Regentin diesen Unsinn nicht zurück? Does not even the presence of our royal regent restrain this folly?

39 muthwillig zertrümmern werden, will wilfully break up, destroy.

40 Bestreben, endeavour.

41 Eures Zeichens? You are by trade?

42 Gnade, daß, &c. It is gracious of you to, &c.

43 übel genug angeschrieben, in bad repute as it is.

44 stänkern, quarrel.

nach Privilegien, und lügen den Neugierigen und Leichtgläubigen was vor, und um eine Kanne Bier[45] bezahlt zu kriegen, fangen sie Händel an, die viel tausend Menschen unglücklich machen. Das ist ihnen eben recht.[46] Wir halten unsre Häuser und Kasten zu gut verwahrt; da möchten sie gern uns mit Feuerbränden davon treiben.

Egmont. Allen Beistand sollt ihr finden; es sind Maßregeln genommen, dem Uebel kräftig zu begegnen.[47] Steht fest gegen die fremde Lehre und glaubt nicht, durch Aufruhr befestige man Privilegien. Bleibt zu Hause; leidet nicht, daß sie sich auf den Straßen rotten.[48] Vernünftige Leute können viel thun.

(Indessen hat sich der größte Haufe verlaufen.)

Zimmermeister. Danken Euer Excellenz, danken für die gute Meinung! Alles was an uns liegt.[49] (Egmont ab.) Ein gnädiger Herr! der echte Niederländer! Gar so nichts Spanisches.

Jetter. Hätten wir ihn nur zum Regenten! Man folgt ihm gerne.

Soest. Das läßt der König wohl sein.[50] Den Platz besetzt er immer mit den Seinigen.

Jetter. Hast du das Kleid gesehen? Das war nach der neusten Art, nach spanischem Schnitt.

Zimmermeister. Ein schöner Herr!

Jetter. Sein Hals wär' ein rechtes Fressen[51] für einen Scharfrichter.[52]

Soest. Bist du toll? was kommt dir ein!

Jetter. Dumm genug, daß einem so was einfällt.[53] — Es

---

[45] Kanne Bier, quart of beer.

[46] Das ist ihnen eben recht, That suits them exactly.

[47] dem Uebel kräftig zu begegnen, to meet the danger; to make a bold stand against the evil.

[48] auf den Straßen rotten, an assembly in the streets.

[49] Alles was an uns liegt, All in our power (we will do).

[50] Das läßt der König wohl sein, The king, I imagine, will not do that.

[51] wär' ein rechtes Fressen, would be a real feast.

[52] Scharfrichter, i.q. sometimes Nachrichter, executioner.

[53] einfällt, has such a thought.

ist mir nun so. Wenn ich einen schönen langen Hals sehe, muß ich gleich wider Willen denken: der ist gut köpfen. — Die verfluchten Executionen! man kriegt sie nicht aus dem Sinne. Wenn die Bursche schwimmen, und ich seh' einen nackten Buckel, gleich fallen sie mir zu Dutzenden ein, die ich habe mit Ruthen streichen sehen.[54] Begegnet mir ein rechter Wanst,[55] mein' ich, den seh' ich schon am Pfahl braten. Des Nachts im Traume zwickt mich's an allen Gliedern; man wird eben keine Stunde froh. Jede Lustbarkeit, jeden Spaß hab' ich bald vergessen; die fürchterlichen Gestalten sind mir wie vor die Stirne gebrannt.

Zweite Scene.

Egmonts Wohnung.

Secretär

(an einem Tisch mit Papieren, er steht unruhig auf).

Er kommt immer nicht! und ich warte schon zwei Stunden, die Feder in der Hand, die Papiere vor mir; und eben heute möcht' ich gern so zeitig fort. Es brennt mir unter den Sohlen.[1] Ich kann vor Ungeduld kaum bleiben. „Sei auf die Stunde da," befahl er mir noch, ehe er wegging; nun kommt er nicht. Es ist so viel zu thun, ich werde vor Mitternacht nicht fertig. Freilich sieht er einem auch einmal durch die Finger.[2] Doch hielt' ich's besser, wenn er strenge wäre und ließe einen auch wieder zur bestimmten Zeit. Man könnte sich einrichten.[3] Von der Regentin ist er nun schon zwei Stunden weg; wer weiß, wen er unterwegs angefaßt hat.

---

[54] mit Ruthen streichen sehen, seen birched with rods.

[55] ein rechter Wanst, a proper stomach.

Second Scene.

[1] Es brennt mir unter den Sohlen, I am eager to be gone; the ground burns under my feet.

[2] durch die Finger sehen, to be indulgent.

[3] sich einrichten, to make arrangements.

Egmont tritt auf.

Wie steht's aus?

Secretär. Ich bin bereit, und drei Boten warten.

Egmont. Ich bin dir wohl zu lang' geblieben; du machst ein verdrießlich Gesicht.[4]

Secretär. Euerm Befehl zu gehorchen, wart' ich schon lange. Hier sind die Papiere!

Egmont. Donna Elvira wird böse auf mich werden,[5] wenn sie hört, daß ich dich abgehalten habe.

Secretär. Ihr scherzt.

Egmont. Nein, nein. Schäme dich nicht. Du zeigst einen guten Geschmack; sie ist hübsch; und es ist mir ganz recht, daß du auf dem Schlosse eine Freundin hast. Was sagen die Briefe?

Secretär. Mancherlei, und wenig Erfreuliches.

Egmont. Da ist gut, daß wir die Freude zu Hause haben und sie nicht auswärts her[6] zu erwarten brauchen. Ist viel gekommen?

Secretär. Genug, und drei Boten warten.

Egmont. Sag' an! das Nöthigste.

Secretär. Es ist alles nöthig.

Egmont. Eins nach dem andern, nur geschwind!

Secretär. Hauptmann Breda schickt die Relation, was weiter in Gent und der umliegenden Gegend vorgefallen. Der Tumult hat sich meistens gelegt. —

Egmont. Er schreibt wohl noch von einzelnen Ungezogenheiten und Tollkühnheiten?[7]

Secretär. Ja! Es kommt noch manches vor.

Egmont. Verschone mich damit.

Secretär. Noch sechs sind eingezogen worden, die bei Ver-

---

[4] ein verdrießlich Gesicht machen, pull a wry face.

[5] wird böse auf mich werden, will be angry with me.

[6] auswärts her, from abroad.

[7] einzelnen Ungezogenheiten und Tollkühnheiten, isolated cases of folly and daring.

wich das Marienbild umgerissen haben. Er fragt an, ob er sie auch wie die andern soll hängen lassen?

Egmont. Ich bin des Hängens müde. Man soll sie durchpeitschen,[8] und sie mögen gehn.

Secretär. Es sind zwei Weiber dabei; soll er die auch durchpeitschen?

Egmont. Die mag er verwarnen und laufen lassen.

Secretär. Brink von Breda's Compagnie will heirathen. Der Hauptmann hofft, ihr werdet's ihm abschlagen.[9] Es sind so viele Weiber bei dem Haufen, schreibt er, daß, wenn wir ausziehen, es keinem Soldatenmarsch, sondern einem Zigeuner-Geschleppe[10] ähnlich sehen wird.

Egmont. Dem mag's noch hingehn![11] Es ist ein schöner junger Kerl; er bat mich noch gar dringend, eh' ich wegging. Aber nun soll's keinem mehr gestattet sein, so leid mir's thut, den armen Teufeln, die ohnedies geplagt genug sind, ihren besten Spaß zu versagen.

Secretär. Einer von den fremden Lehrern ist heimlich durch Comines gegangen und entdeckt worden. Er schwört, er sei im Begriff nach Frankreich zu gehen. Nach dem Befehl soll er enthauptet werden.[12]

Egmont. Sie sollen ihn in der Stille an die Grenze bringen, und ihm versichern, daß er das zweite Mal nicht so wegkommt.[13]

Secretär. Ein Brief von euerm Einnehmer.[14] Er schreibt: es komme wenig Geld ein, er könne auf die Woche die verlangte Summe schwerlich schicken; der Tumult habe in alles die größte Confusion gebracht.

Egmont. Das Geld muß herbei! er mag sehen, wie er es zusammenbringt.

---

[8] Man soll sie durchpeitschen, Have them whipped.

[9] werdet's ihm abschlagen, will refuse him.

[10] ein Zigeuner-Geschleppe, a band of straggling gipsies.

[11] mag's hingehen, let it be conceded.

[12] enthauptet werden, lose his head. By virtue of an edict not long since promulgated, all preachers belonging to Protestant sects were punished by death.

[13] daß er nicht so wegkommt, that he will not get off so cheaply.

[14] Einnehmer, receiver.

Secretär. Er sagt: er werde sein Möglichstes thun und wolle endlich den Raymond, der euch so lange schuldig ist, verklagen und in Verhaft nehmen lassen.

Egmont. Der hat ja versprochen zu bezahlen.

Secretär. Das letzte Mal setzte er sich selbst vierzehn Tage.

Egmont. So gebe man ihm noch vierzehn Tage; und dann mag er gegen ihn verfahren.[15]

Secretär. Ihr thut wohl. Es ist nicht Unvermögen; es ist böser Wille. Er macht gewiß Ernst, wenn er sieht, ihr spaßt nicht. — Ferner sagt der Einnehmer: er wolle den alten Soldaten, den Wittwen und einigen andern, denen ihr Gnadengehalte gebt, die Gebühr[16] einen halben Monat zurückhalten; man könne indessen Rath schaffen; sie möchten sich einrichten.

Egmont. Was ist da einzurichten? Die Leute brauchen das Geld nöthiger als ich. Das soll er bleiben lassen.

Secretär. Woher befehlt ihr denn, daß er das Geld nehmen soll?

Egmont. Darauf mag er denken; es ist ihm im vorigen Briefe schon gesagt.

Secretär. Deßwegen thut er die Vorschläge.

Egmont. Die taugen nicht.[17] Er soll auf was anders sinnen. Er soll Vorschläge thun, die annehmlich sind, und vor allem soll er das Geld schaffen.

Secretär. Ich habe den Brief des Grafen Oliva wieder hierher gelegt. Verzeiht, daß ich euch daran erinnere. Der alte Herr verdient vor allen andern eine ausführliche Antwort.[18] Ihr wolltet ihm selbst schreiben. Gewiß, er liebt euch wie ein Vater.

Egmont. Ich komme nicht dazu. Und unter vielem Verhaßten ist mir das Schreiben das Verhaßteste. Du machst meine Hand ja so gut nach,[19] schreib' in meinem Namen. Ich erwarte

---

[15] verfahren, proceed.

[16] Gnadengehalt, pension; Gebühr, that which is due, sums due.

[17] Die taugen nicht, They are worthless.

[18] ausführliche Antwort, detailed, explicit, answer.

[19] du machst meine Hand so gut

Oranien. Ich komme nicht dazu; und wünschte selbst, daß ihm auf seine Bedenklichkeiten[20] was recht Beruhigendes geschrieben würde.

Secretär. Sagt mir ungefähr eure Meinung; ich will die Antwort schon aufsetzen und sie euch vorlegen. Geschrieben soll sie werden, daß sie vor Gericht für eure Hand gelten kann.

Egmont. Gieb mir den Brief. (Nachdem er hineingesehen.) Guter, ehrlicher Alter! Warst du in deiner Jugend auch wohl so bedächtig? Erstiegst du nie einen Wall? Bliebst du in der Schlacht, wo es die Klugheit anräth, hinten?[21] — Der treue Sorgliche! Er will mein Leben und mein Glück und fühlt nicht, daß der schon todt ist, der um seiner Sicherheit willen lebt. — Schreib' ihm, er möge unbesorgt sein; ich handle wie ich soll, ich werde mich schon wahren;[22] sein Ansehn bei Hofe soll er zu meinen Gunsten brauchen und meines vollkommnen Dankes gewiß sein.

Secretär. Nichts weiter? O, er erwartet mehr.

Egmont. Was soll ich mehr sagen? Willst du mehr Worte machen, so steht's bei dir.[23] Es dreht sich immer um den einen Punkt: ich soll leben, wie ich nicht leben mag. Daß ich fröhlich bin, die Sachen leicht nehme, rasch lebe, das ist mein Glück; und ich vertausch' es nicht gegen die Sicherheit eines Todtengewölbes. Ich habe nun zu der spanischen Lebensart nicht einen Blutstropfen in meinen Adern; nicht Lust, meine Schritte nach der neuen bedächtigen Hof-Cadenz zu mustern.[24] Leb' ich nur, um aufs Leben zu denken? Soll ich den gegenwärtigen Augenblick nicht genießen, damit ich des folgenden gewiß sei? Und diesen wieder mit Sorgen und Grillen verzehren?

---

nach, you imitate my handwriting so well.

[20] Bedenklichkeit, qualms, apprehension.

[21] Bliebst du in der Schlacht, wo es die Klugheit anräth, hinten? Did you remain behind in battle, where prudence counselled you to stay?

[22] wahren, take care of myself.

[23] steht's bei dir, it rests with you.

[24] meine Schritte nach der bedächtigen Hof-Cadenz zu mustern, to measure my steps to suit the careful, slow cadence of the court.

Secretär. Ich bitt' euch, Herr, seid nicht so harsch und rauh gegen den guten Mann. Ihr seid ja sonst gegen alle freundlich. Sagt mir ein gefällig Wort, das den edeln Freund beruhige. Seht, wie sorgfältig er ist, wie leis' er euch berührt.[25]

Egmont. Und doch berührt er immer diese Saite.[26] Er weiß von Alters her, wie verhaßt mir diese Ermahnungen sind; sie machen nur irre, sie helfen nichts. Und wenn ich ein Nachtwandler[27] wäre und auf dem gefährlichen Gipfel eines Hauses spazierte, ist es freundschaftlich, mich beim Namen zu rufen und mich zu warnen, zu wecken und zu tödten? Laßt jeden seines Pfades gehn; er mag sich wahren.

Secretär. Es ziemt euch nicht[28] zu sorgen, aber wer euch kennt und liebt —

Egmont (in den Brief sehend). Da bringt er wieder die alten Mährchen auf, was wir an einem Abend in leichtem Uebermuth der Geselligkeit und des Weins getrieben und gesprochen, und was man daraus für Folgen und Beweise durchs ganze Königreich gezogen und geschleppt habe. — Nun gut! wir haben Schellenkappen, Narrenkutten auf unsrer Diener Aermel sticken lassen[29] und haben diese tolle Zierde nachher in ein Bündel Pfeile

---

[25] wie leis' er euch berührt, how gently he touches you.

[26] doch berührt er immer diese Saite, yet he always harps on that string.

[27] Nachtwandler, moonstruck, somnambulist.

[28] Es ziemt euch nicht, it does not behove you.

[29] Schellenkappen, Narrenkutten auf unserer Diener Aermel sticken lassen. The incident here alluded to took place early in the year 1564. The king's principal financier and agent, Caspar Schetz, Baron of Grobbendonk, gave a dinner-party to a number of noblemen, and the conversation turning upon the Cardinal Granvelle, this ecclesiastic was the theme of much scornful jesting and bitter sarcasm. The pompous display affected by him was turned into well-merited ridicule, and by way of further showing their dislike of the hated ruler, it was proposed to invent at once a livery going to the opposite extreme of plainness, which was to be adopted by the retainers of the noblemen present. The question as to who should invent the costume was left to chance. Dice decided in favour of Egmont, and within a few days afterwards his servants appeared in the new livery, consisting of doublet and hose of coarse grey stuff; a monk's cowl or fool's cap, and bells were embroidered on the long

verwandelt; ein noch gefährlicher Symbol für alle, die deuten wollen, wo nichts zu deuten ist. Wir haben die und jene Thorheit in einem lustigen Augenblick empfangen und geboren; sind schuld, daß eine ganze edle Schaar mit Bettelsäcken und mit einem selbstgewählten Unnamen[30] dem Könige seine Pflicht mit spottender Demuth ins Gedächtniß rief; sind schuld — was ist's nun weiter? Ist ein Fastnachtsspiel gleich Hochverrath?[31] Sind uns die kurzen bunten Lumpen zu mißgönnen, die ein jugendlicher Muth, eine angefrischte Phantasie um unsers Lebens arme Blöße hängen mag? Wenn ihr das Leben gar zu ernsthaft nehmt, was ist denn dran?[32] Wenn uns der Morgen nicht zu neuen Freuden weckt, am Abend uns keine Lust zu hoffen übrig bleibt, ist's wohl des An- und Ausziehens werth? Scheint mir die Sonne heut', um das zu überlegen, was gestern war? und um zu rathen, zu verbinden, was nicht zu errathen, nicht zu verbinden ist, das Schicksal eines kommenden Tages? Schenke mir diese Betrachtungen; wir wollen sie Schülern und Höflingen überlassen. Die mögen sinnen und aussinnen, wandeln und schleichen, gelangen wohin sie können, erschleichen was sie können. — Kannst du von allem diesem etwas brauchen, daß deine Epistel kein Buch wird,

---

hanging sleeves. The success of the quaint device was immense. The duchess laughed at the maker, the cardinal, however, represented to Philip that it was obviously an emblem or symbol of a secret conspiracy. The regent, however, interfered so far as to request them to leave out the monk's cowl, for which a bundle of arrows or a wheatsheaf was substituted.

[30] Bettelsäcken und einem selbstgewählten Unnamen. Count Brederode, with some hundred noblemen, had presented to the regent a petition praying her to intercede with Philip II, to reconsider the recent edicts concerning the Inquisition, stating that they were likely to produce a general rebellion; and after the withdrawal of the deputation, Berlaymont is reported to have said, 'Is it possible that your highness can be afraid of these beggars (gueux)?' The word, overheard by Brederode, was adopted by him as a watchword, and after a banquet given by him to the other members of the deputation, a costume for the confederacy was decided upon; it consisted of a short grey cloak and hose, felt hat, beggar's pouch, and bowl.

[31] Ist ein Fastnachtsspiel gleich Hochverrath? Is a carnival mummery high treason?

[32] was ist denn dran? what is there in it?

so ist mir's recht.[33] Dem guten Alten scheint alles viel zu wichtig. So drückt ein Freund, der lang' unsre Hand gehalten, sie stärker noch einmal, wenn er sie lassen will.

Secretär. Verzeiht mir. Es wird dem Fußgänger schwindlig, der einen Mann mit rasselnder Eile daher fahren sieht.

Egmont. Kind! Kind! nicht weiter! Wie von unsichtbaren Geistern gepeitscht, gehen die Sonnenpferde der Zeit mit unsers Schicksals leichtem Wagen durch;[34] und uns bleibt nichts als,[35] muthig gefaßt, die Zügel festzuhalten, und bald rechts bald links, vom Steine hier, vom Sturze da, die Räder wegzulenken. Wohin es geht, wer weiß es? Erinnert er sich doch kaum, woher er kam!

Secretär. Herr! Herr!

Egmont. Ich stehe hoch und kann und muß noch höher steigen; ich fühle mir[36] Hoffnung, Muth und Kraft. Noch hab' ich meines Wachsthums Gipfel nicht erreicht; und steh' ich droben einst, so will ich fest, nicht ängstlich stehn. Soll ich fallen,[37] so mag ein Donnerschlag, ein Sturmwind, ja ein selbst verfehlter Schritt mich abwärts in die Tiefe stürzen; da lieg' ich mit viel Tausenden. Ich habe nie verschmäht, mit meinen guten Kriegsgesellen um kleinen Gewinnst das blutige Loos zu werfen; und sollt' ich knickern,[38] wenn's um den ganzen freien Werth des Lebens geht?[39]

Secretär. O Herr! Ihr wißt nicht, was für Worte ihr sprecht! Gott erhalt' euch!

Egmont. Nimm deine Papiere zusammen. Oranien kommt. Fertige aus, was am nöthigsten ist, daß die Boten fortkommen, eh' die Thore geschlossen werden. Das andere hat

---

[33] so ist mir's recht, I shall be pleased.

[34] gehen mit unsers Schicksals leichtem Wagen durch, run away with the slight car of our fate.

[35] uns bleibt nichts als, nothing remains for us to do but.

[36] ich fühle mir, I feel within me.

[37] Soll ich fallen, if I am to fall.

[38] sollt' ich knickern? should I be niggardly?

[39] wenn's um . . . geht, when the prize is . . .

Zeit.[40] Den Brief an den Grafen laß bis morgen; versäume nicht Elviren zu besuchen, und grüße sie von mir. — Horche, wie sich die Regentin befindet; sie soll nicht wohl sein, ob sie's gleich verbirgt.

(Secretär ab).

Dritte Scene.

Oranien kommt.

Egmont. Willkommen, Oranien. Ihr scheint mir nicht ganz frei.

Oranien. Was sagt ihr zu unsrer Unterhaltung mit der Regentin?

Egmont. Ich fand in ihrer Art uns aufzunehmen nichts Außerordentliches. Ich habe sie schon öfter so gesehen. Sie schien mir nicht ganz wohl.

Oranien. Merktet ihr nicht, daß sie zurückhaltender[1] war? Erst wollte sie unser Betragen bei dem neuen Aufruhr des Pöbels gelassen billigen; nachher merkte sie an, was sich doch auch für ein falsches Licht darauf werfen lasse; wich dann mit dem Gespräche zu ihrem alten gewöhnlichen Discurs: daß man ihre liebevolle gute Art, ihre Freundschaft zu uns Niederländern nie genug erkannt, zu leicht behandelt habe, daß nichts einen erwünschten Ausgang nehmen wolle, daß sie am Ende wohl müde werden, der König sich zu andern Maaßregeln entschließen müsse. Habt ihr das gehört?

Egmont. Nicht alles; ich dachte unterdessen an was anders. Sie ist ein Weib, guter Oranien, und die möchten immer gern, daß sich alles unter ihr sanftes Joch gelassen schmiegte,[2] daß jeder Hercules die Löwenhaut ablegte und ihren Kunkelhof vermehrte;[3] daß, weil sie friedlich gesinnt sind, die Gährung, die ein Volk

---

[40] das andere hat Zeit, the rest can wait.

Third Scene.

[1] zurückhaltender, more reticent.

[2] alles gelassen schmiegte, everybody quietly submitted to.

[3] ihren Kunkelhof vermehrte, increased her spinster's court. Simile taken from the legend of Hercules and Omphale.

ergreift, der Sturm, den mächtige Nebenbuhler gegen einander erregen, sich durch ein freundlich Wort beilegen ließe, und die widrigsten Elemente sich zu ihren Füßen in sanfter Eintracht vereinigten. Das ist ihr Fall; und da sie es dahin nicht bringen kann, so hat sie keinen Weg als launisch zu werden, sich über Undankbarkeit, Unweisheit zu beklagen, mit schrecklichen Aussichten in die Zukunft zu drohen[4] und zu drohen, daß sie — fortgehen will.

Oranien. Glaubt ihr dasmal nicht, daß sie ihre Drohung erfüllt?

Egmont. Nimmermehr! Wie oft habe ich sie schon reisefertig gesehn! Wo will sie denn hin? Hier Statthalterin, Königin; glaubst du, daß sie es unterhalten wird,[5] am Hofe ihres Bruders unbedeutende Tage abzuhaspeln?[6] oder nach Italien zu gehen und sich in alten Familienverhältnissen herumzuschleppen?[7]

Oranien. Man hält sie dieser Entschließung nicht fähig, weil ihr sie habt zaudern, weil ihr sie habt zurücktreten sehen; dennoch liegt's wohl in ihr;[8] neue Umstände treiben sie zu dem lang' verzögerten Entschluß. Wenn sie ginge? und der König schickte einen andern?

Egmont. Nun, der würde kommen und würde eben auch zu thun finden. Mit großen Planen, Projecten und Gedanken würde er kommen, wie er alles zurecht rücken,[9] unterwerfen und zusammenhalten wolle; und würde heut' mit dieser Kleinigkeit, morgen mit einer andern zu thun haben, übermorgen jene Hinderniß finden, einen Monat mit Entwürfen,[10] einen andern mit

---

[4] mit schrecklichen Aussichten zu drohen, to threaten dire consequences.

[5] unterhalten wird, will bear.

[6] am Hofe ihres Bruders unbedeutende Tage abzuhaspeln, to spend her days in insignificance at her brother's court.

[7] oder nach Italien zu gehen und sich in alten Familienverhältnissen herumzuschleppen? or go to Italy, and meddle with old family concerns?

[8] zurücktreten sehen, seen her reconsider her resolution; dennoch liegt's wohl in ihr, yet she is quite capable of it.

[9] zurecht rücken, put to rights.

[10] einen Monat mit Entwürfen zubringen, pass one month in making plans.

Verdruß über fehlgeschlagne Unternehmen, ein halb Jahr in Sorgen über eine einzige Provinz zubringen. Auch ihm wird die Zeit vergehn, der Kopf schwindeln, und die Dinge wie zuvor ihren Gang halten,[11] daß er, statt weite Meere nach einer vorgezogenen Linie zu durchsegeln, Gott danken mag, wenn er sein Schiff in diesem Sturme vom Felsen hält.

Oranien. Wenn man nun aber dem König zu einem Versuch riethe?[12]

Egmont. Der wäre?

Oranien. Zu sehen, was der Rumpf ohne Haupt anfinge.

Egmont. Wie?

Oranien. Egmont, ich trage viele Jahre her alle unsre Verhältnisse am Herzen, ich stehe immer wie über einem Schachspiele und halte keinen Zug des Gegners für unbedeutend;[13] und wie müßige Menschen mit der größten Sorgfalt sich um die Geheimnisse der Natur bekümmern, so halt' ich es für Pflicht, für Beruf eines Fürsten, die Gesinnungen, die Rathschläge aller Parteien zu kennen. Ich habe Ursach', einen Ausbruch zu befürchten. Der König hat lange nach gewissen Grundsätzen gehandelt; er sieht, daß er damit nicht auskommt;[14] was ist wahrscheinlicher, als daß er es auf einem andern Wege versucht?

Egmont. Ich glaub's nicht. Wenn man alt wird und hat so viel versucht, und es will in der Welt nie zur Ordnung kommen, muß man es endlich wohl genug haben.

Oranien. Eins hat er noch nicht versucht.

Egmont. Nun?

Oranien. Das Volk zu schonen und die Fürsten zu verderben.[15]

---

[11] die Dinge wie zuvor ihren Gang halten, matters go on as before.

[12] zu einem Versuch riethe, counsel an attempt.

[13] ich stehe immer wie über einem Schachspiele und halte keinen Zug des Gegners für unbedeutend, I watch continually, as it were, the chessboard, and deem no move of my opponent insignificant.

[14] daß er damit nicht auskommt, that he will not succeed; that they will not suffice.

[15] die Fürsten zu verderben, to destroy the princes.

Egmont. Wie viele haben das schon lange gefürchtet! Es ist keine Sorge.

Oranien. Sonst war's Sorge, nach und nach ist mir's Vermuthung, zuletzt Gewißheit geworden.[16]

Egmont. Und hat der König treuere Diener als uns?

Oranien. Wir dienen ihm auf unsre Art; und unter einander können wir gestehen, daß wir des Königs Rechte und die unsrigen wohl abzuwägen wissen.[17]

Egmont. Wer thut's nicht? Wir sind ihm unterthan und gewärtig in dem, was ihm zukommt.[18]

Oranien. Wenn er sich nun aber mehr zuschriebe und Treulosigkeit nennte, was wir heißen auf unsre Rechte halten?

Egmont. Wir werden uns vertheidigen können. Er rufe die Ritter des Vließes zusammen, wir wollen uns richten lassen.

Oranien. Und was wäre ein Urtheil vor der Untersuchung? eine Strafe vor dem Urtheil?

Egmont. Eine Ungerechtigkeit, der sich Philipp nie schuldig machen wird; und eine Thorheit, die ich ihm und seinen Räthen nicht zutraue.[19]

Oranien. Und wenn sie nun ungerecht und thöricht wären?

Egmont. Nein, Oranien, es ist nicht möglich. Wer sollte wagen Hand an uns zu legen? — Uns gefangen zu nehmen, wär' ein verlornes und fruchtloses Unternehmen. Nein, sie wagen nicht, das Panier der Tyrannei so hoch aufzustecken. Der Windhauch, der diese Nachricht übers Land brächte, würde ein ungeheures Feuer zusammentreiben. Und wo hinaus wollten sie?[20] Richten und verdammen kann nicht der König allein; und

---

[16] Sonst war's Sorge, nach und nach ist mir's Vermuthung, zuletzt Gewißheit geworden, At first it was but apprehension; gradually it has grown surmise, and at last become certainty.

[17] unter einander können wir gestehen, daß wir des Königs Rechte und die unsrigen wohl abzuwägen wissen, between ourselves we may (as well) confess that we know how to weigh the king's prerogative and our own.

[18] gewärtig in dem, was ihm zukommt, obey in all things lawful.

[19] die ich ihm und seinen Räthen nicht zutraue, which I do not think him and his advisers capable of.

[20] Und wo hinaus wollten sie? And how far would they go?

wollten sie meuchelmörderisch an unser Leben?[21] — Sie können nicht wollen. Ein schrecklicher Bund würde in einem Augenblick das Volk vereinigen. Haß und ewige Trennung vom spanischen Namen würde sich gewaltsam erklären.

Oranien. Die Flamme wüthete dann über unserm Grabe, und das Blut unsrer Feinde flösse zum leeren Sühnopfer.[22] Laß uns denken, Egmont.

Egmont. Wie sollten sie aber?

Oranien. Alba ist unterwegs.[23]

Egmont. Ich glaub's nicht.

Oranien. Ich weiß es.

Egmont. Die Regentin wollte nichts wissen.

Oranien. Um desto mehr bin ich überzeugt. Die Regentin wird ihm Platz machen. Seinen Mordsinn kenn' ich, und ein Heer bringt er mit.

Egmont. Aufs neue die Provinzen zu belästigen? Das Volk wird höchst schwierig werden.

Oranien. Man wird sich der Häupter versichern.[24]

Egmont. Nein! Nein!

Oranien. Laß uns gehen, jeder in seine Provinz. Dort wollen wir uns verstärken; mit offner Gewalt fängt er nicht an.

Egmont. Müssen wir ihn nicht begrüßen, wenn er kommt?

Oranien. Wir zögern.

Egmont. Und wenn er uns im Namem des Königs bei seiner Ankunft fordert?

Oranien. Suchen wir Ausflüchte.

Egmont. Und wenn er dringt?

Oranien. Entschuldigen wir uns.

Egmont. Und wenn er drauf besteht?

Oranien. Kommen wir um so weniger.

Egmont. Und der Krieg ist erklärt, und wir sind die Re-

---

21 Und wollten sie meuchelmörderisch an unser Leben? And do they intend to assassinate us?

22 flösse zum leeren Sühnopfer, would flow a vain propitiatory sacrifice.

23 unterwegs, on the road here.

24 sich der Häupter versichern, make sure of the heads.

bellen. Oranien, laß dich nicht durch Klugheit verführen;[25] ich weiß, daß Furcht dich nicht weichen macht. Bedenke den Schritt.

Oranien. Ich hab' ihn bedacht.

Egmont. Bedenke, wenn du dich irrst, woran du schuld bist: an dem verderblichsten Kriege, der je ein Land verwüstet hat. Dein Weigern ist das Signal, das die Provinzen mit einem Male zu den Waffen ruft, das jede Grausamkeit rechtfertigt, wozu Spanien von jeher nur gern den Vorwand gehascht hat.[26] Was wir lange mühselig gestillt haben, wirst du mit einem Winke zur schrecklichsten Verwirrung aufhetzen. Denk' an die Städte, die Edeln, das Volk, an die Handlung, den Feldbau, die Gewerbe! und denke die Verwüstung, den Mord! — Ruhig sieht der Soldat wohl im Felde seinen Kameraden neben sich hinfallen; aber den Fluß herunter werden dir die Leichen der Bürger, der Kinder, der Jungfrauen entgegenschwimmen,[27] daß du mit Entsetzen dastehst und nicht mehr weißt, wessen Sache du vertheidigst, da die zu Grunde gehen, für deren Freiheit du die Waffen ergreifst. Und wie wird dir's sein, wenn du dir still sagen mußt: Für meine Sicherheit ergriff ich sie!

Oranien. Wir sind nicht einzelne Menschen, Egmont. Ziemt es sich, uns für Tausende hinzugeben, so ziemt es sich auch, uns für Tausende zu schonen.

Egmont. Wer sich schont, muß sich selbst verdächtig werden.

Oranien. Wer sich kennt, kann sicher vor- und rückwärts gehen.

Egmont. Das Uebel, das du fürchtest, wird gewiß durch deine That.

Oranien. Es ist klug und kühn, dem unvermeidlichen Uebel entgegenzugehen.[28]

---

[25] laß dich nicht durch Klugheit verführen, be not led astray by thy wisdom.

[26] wozu Spanien von jeher nur gern den Vorwand gehascht hat, to employ which (i. e. cruelty) Spain has at all times caught at every excuse.

[27] den Fluß herunter werden dir die Leichen der Bürger, der Kinder, der Jungfrauen entgegenschwimmen, the corpses of citizens, children, and maidens, will swim down the river and meet you.

[28] Es ist klug und kühn, dem unvermeidlichen Uebel entgegenzugehen, It is prudent and bold to meet halfway inevitable evil.

Egmont. Bei so großer Gefahr kommt die leichteste Hoffnung in Anschlag.[29]

Oranien. Wir haben nicht für den leisesten Fußtritt Platz mehr; der Abgrund liegt hart vor uns.[30]

Egmont. Ist des Königs Gunst ein so schmaler Grund?

Oranien. So schmal nicht, aber schlüpfrig.

Egmont. Bei Gott! man thut ihm Unrecht. Ich mag nicht leiden, daß man unwürdig von ihm denkt! Er ist Carls Sohn und keiner Niedrigkeit fähig.[31]

Oranien. Die Könige thun nichts Niedriges.

Egmont. Man sollte ihn kennen lernen.

Oranien. Eben diese Kenntniß räth' uns, eine gefährliche Probe nicht abzuwarten.

Egmont. Keine Probe ist gefährlich, zu der man Muth hat.

Oranien. Du wirst aufgebracht, Egmont.

Egmont. Ich muß mit meinen Augen sehen.

Oranien. O säh'st du diesmal nur mit den meinigen! Freund! weil du sie offen hast, glaubst du, du siehst. Ich gehe! Warte du Alba's Ankunft ab, und Gott sei bei dir! Vielleicht rettet dich mein Weigern. Vielleicht, daß der Drache nichts zu fangen glaubt, wenn er uns nicht beide auf einmal verschlingt.[32] Vielleicht zögert er, um seinen Anschlag sicherer auszuführen; und vielleicht siehest du indeß die Sache in ihrer wahren Gestalt. Aber dann schnell! Rette! rette dich! — Leb' wohl! — Laß deiner Aufmerksamkeit nichts entgehen:[33] wie viel Mannschaft er mitbringt, wie er die Stadt besetzt, was für Macht die Regentin behält, wie deine Freunde gefaßt sind.[34] Gieb mir Nachricht — — — Egmont —

---

[29] kommt die leiseste Hoffnung in Anschlag, the slightest hope is of moment.

[30] liegt hart vor uns, lies close before us, hard by.

[31] keiner Niedrigkeit fähig, capable of no mean act.

[32] Vielleicht, daß der Drache nichts zu fangen glaubt, wenn er uns nicht beide auf einmal verschlingt, Perhaps the dragon may not think he has caught anything unless he swallows us both at once.

[33] Laß nichts entgehen, Let nothing escape.

[34] wie deine Freunde gefaßt sind, how your friends are disposed.

Egmont. Was willst du?

Oranien (ihn bei der Hand fassend). Laß dich überreden! Geh' mit!

Egmont. Wie? Thränen, Oranien?

Oranien. Einen Verlornen zu beweinen, ist auch männlich.

Egmont. Du wähnst mich verloren?

Oranien. Du bist's. Bedenke! Dir bleibt nur eine kurze Frist. Leb' wohl!

(Ab.)

Egmont (allein). Daß andrer Menschen Gedanken solchen Einfluß auf uns haben! Mir wär' es nie eingekommen;[35] und dieser Mann trägt seine Sorglichkeit in mich herüber. — Weg! — Das ist eine fremder Tropfen in meinem Blute. Gute Natur, wirf ihn wieder heraus! Und von meiner Stirne die sinnenden Runzeln wegzubaden,[36] giebt es ja wohl noch ein freundlich Mittel.

---

[35] Mir wär' es nie eingekommen, It would never have entered my head.

[36] von meiner Stirne die sinnenden Runzeln wegzubaden, to smooth from my forehead the wrinkles of care.

To understand the previous scene, it must be borne in mind that William of Orange had for a long time held watch over the King of Spain, and, through a host of spies, had learned all that was transacted in the king's council.

This information not only tallied with the reports sent from Spain by Bergen and Montigny but was also fully borne out by an intercepted letter of the Spanish ambassador in France to the regent. The means proposed to meet the evil, frustrated by the refusal of Egmont, were to at once negotiate a defensive alliance with all the Protestants in France, Switzerland, and Germany, and to raise in the empire 4,000 horse, with a proportionate body of infantry.

Dritter Aufzug.

Erste Scene.

Palast der Regentin.

Margarete von Parma.

Ich hätte mir's vermuthen sollen.[1] Ha! Wenn man in Mühe und Arbeit vor sich hinlebt, denkt man immer, man thue das Möglichste; und der von weitem zusieht und befiehlt, glaubt, er verlange nur das Mögliche. — O die Könige! — Ich hätte nicht geglaubt, daß es mich so verdrießen könnte.[2] Es ist so schön, zu herrschen! — Und abzudanken? — Ich weiß nicht, wie mein Vater es konnte; aber ich will es auch.

Machiavell erscheint im Grunde.

Regentin. Tretet näher, Machiavell. Ich denke hier über den Brief meines Bruders.

Machiavell. Ich darf wissen, was er enthält?

Regentin. So viel zärtliche Aufmerksamkeit für mich, als Sorgfalt für seine Staaten. Er rühmt die Standhaftigkeit, den Fleiß und die Treue, womit ich bisher für die Rechte seiner Majestät in diesen Landen gewacht habe. Er bedauert mich, daß mir das unbändige Volk so viel zu schaffen mache.[3] Er ist von der Tiefe meiner Einsichten so vollkommen überzeugt, mit der Klugheit meines Betragens so außerordentlich zufrieden, daß ich fast

---

[1] Ich hätte mir's vermuthen sollen, I ought to have suspected it.

[2] daß es mich so verdrießen könnte, that it could vex me so much.

[3] daß mir das unbändige Volk so viel zu schaffen mache, that the unruly people gave me so much trouble.

sagen muß, der Brief ist für einen König zu schön geschrieben, für einen Bruder gewiß.

Machiavell. Es ist nicht das erstemal, daß er euch seine gerechte Zufriedenheit bezeigt.[4]

Regentin. Aber das erstemal, daß es rednerische Figur ist.

Machiavell. Ich versteh' euch nicht.

Regentin. Ihr werdet. — Denn er meint nach diesem Eingange: ohne Mannschaft, ohne eine kleine Armee werde ich immer hier eine üble Figur spielen![5] Wir hätten, sagt er, unrecht gethan, auf die Klagen der Einwohner unsre Soldaten aus den Provinzen zu ziehen. Eine Besatzung, meint er, die dem Bürger auf dem Nacken lastet, verbiete ihm durch ihre Schwere, große Sprünge zu machen.[6]

Machiavell. Es würde die Gemüther äußerst aufbringen.

Regentin. Der König meint aber, hörst du? — Er meint, daß ein tüchtiger General, so einer, der gar keine Raison annimmt, gar bald mit Volk und Adel, Bürgern und Bauern fertig werden könne;[7] — und schickt deßwegen mit einem starken Heere — den Herzog von Alba.

Machiavell. Alba?

Regentin. Du wunderst dich?

Machiavell. Ihr sagt: er schickt. Er fragt wohl, ob er schicken soll?

Regentin. Der König fragt nicht; er schickt.

Machiavell. So werdet ihr einen erfahrnen Krieger in euern Diensten haben.[8]

---

[4] daß er euch seine gerechte Zufriedenheit bezeigt, that he manifests his just contentment.

[5] werde ich immer hier eine üble Figur spielen, I should always play but a sorry part.

[6] verbiete ihm durch ihre Schwere, große Sprünge zu machen, by its weight prevent their (lit. making great jumps) being haughty and rebellious.

[7] gar bald mit Volk und Adel, Bürgern und Bauern fertig werden könne, soon bring people and nobility, citizens and peasantry, to reason.

[8] So werdet ihr einen erfahrnen Krieger in euern Diensten haben, You will have an experienced soldier in your service. The Duke of Alba was born 1508; when only sixteen, he served under the Constable of Castille against France, and dis-

Regentin. In meinen Diensten? Rede gerad' heraus, Machiavell.

Machiavell. Ich möcht' euch nicht vorgreifen.[9]

Regentin. Und ich möchte mich verstellen.[10] Es ist mir empfindlich, sehr empfindlich. Ich wollte lieber, mein Bruder sagte, wie er's denkt, als daß er förmliche Episteln unterschreibt, die ein Staatssecretär aufsetzt.[11]

Machiavell. Sollte man nicht einsehen? —

Regentin. Und ich kenne sie inwendig und auswendig. Sie möchten's gern gesäubert und gekehrt haben; und weil sie selbst nicht zugreifen, so findet ein jeder Vertrauen, der mit dem Besen in der Hand kommt. O, mir ist's, als wenn ich den König und sein Conseil auf dieser Tapete gewirkt sähe.

Machiavell. So lebhaft?

Regentin. Es fehlt kein Zug. Es sind gute Menschen drunter. Der ehrliche Rodrich,[12] der so erfahren und mäßig ist, nicht zu hoch will und doch nichts fallen läßt, der gerade Alonzo, der fleißige Freneda, der feste Las Vargas, und noch einige, die mitgehen, wenn die gute Partei mächtig wird. Da sitzt aber der

---

tinguished himself at the taking of Fontarabia, no less than in the following year in the battle of Pavia. In 1527, he served in Hungary against Solyman, and his name recurs occasionally in the following few years. In 1542, he held out in Perpignan against the French. In 1546, he was imperial generalissimo in Germany, and gained the important battle of Mühlberg. At the moment of the Emperor Charles V.'s abdication, he was commander of the imperial armies in Italy, and kept Francis de Guise in check. After the peace of Cateau Cambresis, he, Orange, and Egmont were the hostages demanded by Henry II., after whose death he was sent into the Netherlands as successor to Margaret of Parma.

[9] vorgreifen, anticipate.

[10] verstellen, dissemble.

[11] die ein Staatssecretär aufsetzt, which a secretary of state has penned.

[12] This nobleman was Ruy Gomes de Silva, Prince of Eboli, who had been early received into the royal household, where his amiable disposition and great tact soon made him a favourite of both Charles and Philip. The influence which he exercised over the latter is not inaptly described by the punning title of 'Rey Gomes.' The Duke of Alva, his rival, remarked of him:—'Ruy Gomes, though not the greatest statesman that ever lived, was such a master in the knowledge of the

hohläugige Toledaner[13] mit der ehernen Stirne und dem tiefen Feuerblick, murmelt zwischen den Zähnen von Weibergüte, unzeitigem Nachgeben, und daß Frauen wohl von zugerittenen Pferden sich tragen lassen,[14] selbst aber schlechte Stallmeister sind, und solche Späße, die ich ehmals von den politischen Herren habe mit durchhören müssen.

Machiavell. Ihr habt zu dem Gemälde einen guten Farbentopf gewählt.

Regentin. Gesteht nur, Machiavell: In meiner ganzen Schattirung,[15] aus der ich allenfalls malen könnte, ist kein Ton so gelbbraun, gallenschwarz, wie Alba's Gesichtsfarbe und als die Farbe, aus der er malt. Jeder ist bei ihm gleich ein Gotteslästerer, ein Majestätsschänder: denn aus diesem Kapitel kann man sie alle sogleich rädern, pfählen, viertheilen und verbrennen.[16] — Das Gute, was ich hier gethan habe, sieht gewiß in der Ferne wie nichts aus, eben weil's gut ist. — Da hängt er sich an jeden Muthwillen,[17] der vorbei ist, erinnert an jede Unruhe, die gestillt ist; und es wird dem Könige vor den Augen so voll Meuterei, Aufruhr und Tollkühnheit, daß er sich vorstellt, sie fräßen sich hier einander auf, wenn eine flüchtig vorübergehende Ungezogenheit[18] eines rohen Volks bei uns lange vergessen ist. Da faßt er einen recht herzlichen Haß auf die armen Leute; sie kommen

---

humours and dispositions of kings that we were all of us fools in comparison.' (Prescott, quoting Bermudes de Castro.) In the king's council, when the question of how to deal with the disturbed provinces was raised, Ruy Gomez deprecated all severe measures, assuring the king that the best way to win the affections of the people was *clemency*. In this view he was supported by the secretary, Antonio Perez, and the former ambassador in England, the Duke of Feria; while Alva and the grand-inquisitor, Cardinal Espinosa, advocated an immediate crusade against the heretics.

[13] der hohläugige Toledaner, the hollow-eyed Toledan, i.e. Alba.

[14] von zugerittenen Pferden sich tragen lassen, can ride broken-in horses.

[15] Schattirung, colouring.

[16] rädern, pfählen, viertheilen und verbrennen, break on the wheel, empale, quarter, and burn.

[17] hängt er sich an jeden Muthwillen, he dwells on every foolish prank.

[18] flüchtig vorübergehende Ungezogenheit, a mere passing rudeness.

ihm abscheulich, ja wie Thiere und Ungeheuer vor, er sieht sich nach Feuer und Schwert um und wähnt, so bändige man Menschen.[19]

Machiavell. Ihr scheint mir zu heftig, ihr nehmt die Sache zu hoch. Bleibt ihr nicht Regentin?

Regentin. Das kenn' ich. Er wird eine Instruction bringen. — Ich bin in Staatsgeschäften alt genug geworden, um zu wissen, wie man einen verdrängt, ohne ihm seine Bestallung zu nehmen.[20] — Erst wird er eine Instruction bringen, die wird unbestimmt und schief sein;[21] er wird um sich greifen,[22] denn er hat die Gewalt, und wenn ich mich beklage, wird er eine geheime Instruction vorschützen;[23] wenn ich sie sehen will, wird er mich herumziehen;[24] wenn ich drauf bestehe, wird er mir ein Papier zeigen, das ganz was anders enthält; und wenn ich mich da nicht beruhige, gar nicht mehr thun, als wenn ich redete.[25] — Indeß wird er, was ich fürchte, gethan, und was ich wünsche, weit abwärts gelenkt haben.

Machiavell. Ich wollt', ich könnt' euch widersprechen.

Regentin. Was ich mit unsäglicher Geduld beruhigte, wird er durch Härte und Grausamkeit wieder aufhetzen;[26] ich werde vor meinen Augen mein Werk verloren sehn und überdies noch seine Schuld zu tragen haben.

Machiavell. Erwarten's Eure Hoheit.

Regentin. So viel Gewalt hab' ich über mich,[27] um stille

---

[19] wähnt, so bändige man Menschen, imagines one could tame men thus.

[20] wie man einen verdrängt, ohne ihm seine Bestallung zu nehmen, how one may supplant another without [actually] depriving him of his office.

[21] wird unbestimmt und schief sein, is probably vague and ambiguous.

[22] er wird um sich greifen, he will become arrogant.

[23] wird er eine geheime Instruction vorschützen, he will shield himself behind secret instructions.

[24] wird er mich herumziehen, he will put me off.

[25] gar nicht mehr thun, als wenn ich redete, will take no notice of my speaking.

[26] aufhetzen, enrage, excite; irritate.

[27] So viel Gewalt habe ich über mich, I have so much power over myself.

zu sein. Laß ihn kommen; ich werde ihm mit der besten Art Platz machen,[28] eh' er mich verdrängt.

Machiavell. So rasch diesen wichtigen Schritt?

Regentin. Schwerer als du denkst. Wer zu herrschen gewohnt ist, wer's hergebracht hat,[29] daß jeden Tag das Schicksal von Tausenden in seiner Hand liegt, steigt vom Throne wie ins Grab. Aber besser so, als einem Gespenste gleich unter den Lebenden bleiben und mit hohlem Ansehn einen Platz behaupten wollen, den ihm ein anderer abgeerbt hat[30] und nun besitzt und genießt.

Zweite Scene.

Clärchens Wohnung.

Clärchen. Mutter.

Mutter. So eine Liebe wie Brackenburgs hab' ich nie gesehen; ich glaubte, sie sei nur in Heldengeschichten.[1]

Clärchen (geht in der Stube auf und ab, ein Lied zwischen den Lippen summend).

Glücklich allein
Ist die Seele, die liebt.

Mutter. Er vermuthet deinen Umgang mit Egmont; und ich glaube, wenn du ihm ein wenig freundlich thätest,[2] wenn du wolltest, er heirathete dich noch.

Clärchen (singt).

Freudvoll
Und leidvoll,
Gedankenvoll sein;

---

[28] mit der besten Art Platz machen, will make way for him with good grace.

[29] wer's hergebracht hat, who is used to.

[30] den ihm ein anderer abgeerbt hat, that another has inherited.

Second Scene.

[1] sie sei nur in Heldengeschichten, it was to be found only in romances.

[2] wenn du ihm ein wenig freundlich thätest, if you were but a little kind to him.

Hangen
Und bangen
In schwebender Pein;
Himmelhoch jauchzend,
Zum Tode betrübt;
Glücklich allein
Ist die Seele, die liebt.

Mutter. Laß das Heiopopeio.[3]

Clärchen. Scheltet mir's nicht; es ist ein kräftig Lied. Hab' ich doch schon manchmal ein großes Kind damit schlafen gewiegt.[4]

Mutter. Du hast doch nichts im Kopfe als deine Liebe. Vergäßest du nur nicht alles über das Eine. Den Brackenburg solltest du in Ehren halten, sag' ich dir. Er kann dich noch einmal glücklich machen.

Clärchen. Er?

Mutter. O ja! es kommt eine Zeit! — Ihr Kinder seht nichts voraus und überhorcht unsre Erfahrungen.[5] Die Jugend und die schöne Liebe, alles hat sein Ende; und es kommt eine Zeit, wo man Gott dankt, wenn man irgendwo unterkriechen kann.[6]

Clärchen (schaudert, schweigt und fährt auf). Mutter, laßt die Zeit kommen wie den Tod. Dran vorzudenken ist schreckhaft! — Und wenn er kommt! Wenn wir müssen — dann wollen wir uns geberden, wie wir können — Egmont, ich dich entbehren! — (In Thränen.) Nein, es ist nicht möglich, nicht möglich.

Egmont in einem Reitermantel, den Hut ins Gesicht gedrückt.

Clärchen!

Clärchen (thut einen Schrei, fährt zurück). Egmont! (Sie eilt auf ihn zu.) Egmont! (Sie umarmt ihn und ruht an ihm.) O du guter, lieber, süßer! Kommst du? bist du da?

Egmont. Guten Abend, Mutter!

---

[3] Laß das Heiopopeio, Leave off that baby's song.

[4] schlafen gewiegt, rocked asleep (a grown-up child, i.e. Egmont).

[5] überhorcht unsere Erfahrungen, pay no heed to our experience.

[6] wenn man irgendwo unterkriechen kann, if one can find a shelter somewhere.

Mutter. Gott grüß' euch, edler Herr! Meine Kleine ist fast vergangen, daß ihr so lang ausbleibt;[7] sie hat wieder den ganzen Tag von euch geredet und gesungen.

Egmont. Ihr gebt mir doch ein Nachtessen?

Mutter. Zu viel Gnade. Wenn wir nur etwas hätten!

Clärchen. Freilich! Seid nur ruhig, Mutter; ich habe schon alles darauf eingerichtet,[8] ich habe etwas zubereitet. Verrathet mich nicht, Mutter.

Mutter. Schmal genug.[9]

Clärchen. Wartet nur! Und dann denk' ich: wenn er bei mir ist, hab' ich gar keinen Hunger; da sollte er auch keinen großen Appetit haben, wenn ich bei ihm bin.

Egmont. Meinst du?

Clärchen (stampft mit dem Fuße und kehrt sich unwillig um).

Egmont. Wie ist dir?

Clärchen. Wie seid ihr heute so kalt! Ihr habt mir noch keinen Kuß angeboten. Warum habt ihr die Arme in den Mantel gewickelt, wie ein Wochenkind?[10] Ziemt keinem Soldaten noch Liebhaber, die Arme eingewickelt zu haben.

Egmont. Zu Zeiten, Liebchen, zu Zeiten. Wenn der Soldat auf der Lauer steht und dem Feinde etwas ablisten möchte, da nimmt er sich zusammen, faßt sich selbst in seine Arme und kaut seinen Anschlag reif.[11] Und ein Liebhaber —

Mutter. Wollt ihr euch nicht setzen? es euch nicht bequem machen? Ich muß in die Küche, Clärchen denkt an nichts, wenn ihr da seid. Ihr müßt fürlieb nehmen.[12]

Egmont. Euer guter Wille ist die beste Würze.[13]

(Mutter ab).

---

[7] ist fast vergangen, daß ihr so lange ausbleibt, has almost gone out of her mind because you stayed away so long.

[8] ich habe schon alles darauf eingerichtet, I have got everything ready.

[9] Schmal genug, It is little enough.

[10] wie ein Wochenkind, like a new-born babe.

[11] kaut seinen Anschlag reif, matures his plans.

[12] Ihr müßt fürlieb nehmen, You must be satisfied, put up, with what there is.

[13] ist die beste Würze, is the best condiment.

Clärchen. Und was wär' denn meine Liebe?

Egmont. So viel du willst.

Clärchen. Vergleicht sie, wenn ihr das Herz habt.

Egmont. Zuvörderst also.[14] (Er wirft den Mantel ab und steht in einem prächtigen Kleide da.)

Clärchen. O je!

Egmont. Nun hab' ich die Arme frei. (Er herzt sie.)

Clärchen. Laßt! Ihr verderbt euch. (Sie tritt zurück.) Wie prächtig! Da darf ich euch nicht anrühren.

Egmont. Bist du zufrieden? Ich versprach dir, einmal Spanisch zu kommen.

Clärchen. Ich bat euch zeither nicht mehr drum; ich dachte, ihr wolltet nicht — Ach und das goldne Vließ![15]

Egmont. Da siehst du's nun.

Clärchen. Das hat dir der Kaiser umgehängt?

Egmont. Ja, Kind! und Kette und Zeichen geben dem, der sie trägt, die edelsten Freiheiten. Ich erkenne auf Erden keinen Richter über meine Handlungen, als den Großmeister des Ordens mit dem versammelten Kapitel der Ritter.

Clärchen. O, du dürftest die ganze Welt über dich richten lassen. — Der Sammet ist gar zu herrlich, und die Passement-Arbeit![16] und das Gestickte! — Man weiß nicht, wo man anfangen soll.

Egmont. Sieh dich nur satt.[17]

Clärchen. Und das goldne Vließ! Ihr erzähltet mir die Geschichte und sagtet: es sei ein Zeichen alles Großen[18] und Kostbaren, was man mit Müh' und Fleiß verdient und erwirbt. Es

---

[14] Zuvörderst also, First and foremost, then.

[15] und das goldne Vließ! and the Golden Fleece. The Order was founded in 1430 by Duke Philip III. of Burgundy, at his marriage with Isabella of Portugal. It consisted originally of a chapter of twenty-four knights, which number was increased by seven in 1431, and by Charles V. raised to fifty. For the privileges conferred, vide note below.

[16] Passement-Arbeit, trimmings.

[17] Sieh dich nur satt, Feast your eyes on it.

[18] es sei ein Zeichen alles Großen, it were a mark of all that is great.

ist sehr kostbar — ich kann's deiner Liebe vergleichen. — Ich trage sie eben so am Herzen — und hernach —

Egmont. Was willst du sagen?

Clärchen. Hernach vergleicht sich's auch wieder nicht.[19]

Egmont. Wie so?

Clärchen. Ich habe sie nicht mit Müh' und Fleiß erworben, nicht verdient.

Egmont. In der Liebe ist es anders. Du verdienst sie, weil du dich nicht darum bewirbst — und die Leute erhalten sie auch meist allein, die nicht darnach jagen.

Clärchen. Hast du das von dir abgenommen?[20] Hast du diese stolze Anmerkung über dich selbst gemacht? du, den alles Volk liebt?

Egmont. Hätt' ich nur etwas für sie gethan! könnt' ich etwas für sie thun! Es ist ihr guter Wille, mich zu lieben.

Clärchen. Du warst gewiß heute bei der Regentin?

Egmont. Ich war bei ihr.

Clärchen. Bist du gut mit ihr?[21]

Egmont. Es sieht einmal so aus. Wir sind einander freundlich und dienstlich.

Clärchen. Und im Herzen?

Egmont. Will ich ihr wohl. Jedes hat seine eignen Absichten. Das thut nichts zur Sache. Sie ist eine treffliche Frau, kennt ihre Leute, und sähe tief genug, wenn sie auch nicht argwöhnisch wäre. Ich mache ihr viel zu schaffen,[22] weil sie hinter meinem Betragen immer Geheimnisse sucht und ich keine habe.

Clärchen. So gar keine?

Egmont. Eh nun! einen kleinen Hinterhalt. Jeder Wein setzt Weinstein in den Fässern an[23] mit der Zeit. Oranien ist

---

[19] Hernach vergleicht sich's auch wieder nicht, Then the simile does not apply.

[20] Hast du das von dir abgenommen? Have you experienced that yourself?

[21] Bist du gut mit ihr? Are you on good terms with her?

[22] Ich mache ihr viel zu schaffen, I cause her much trouble.

[23] Jeder Wein setzt Weinstein in den Fässern an, Every kind of wine deposits tartar in the casks.

doch noch eine bessere Unterhaltung für sie[24] und eine immer neue Aufgabe. Er hat sich in den Credit gesetzt, daß er immer etwas Geheimes vorhabe: und nun sieht sie immer nach seiner Stirne, was er wohl denken, auf seine Schritte, wohin er sie wohl richten möchte.

Clärchen. Verstellt sie sich?[25]

Egmont. Regentin, und du fragst?

Clärchen. Verzeiht, ich wollte fragen: ist sie falsch?

Egmont. Nicht mehr und nicht weniger als jeder, der seine Absichten erreichen will.

Clärchen. Ich könnte mich in die Welt nicht finden.[26] Sie hat aber auch einen männlichen Geist, sie ist ein ander Weib als wir Nätherinnen und Köchinnen. Sie ist groß, herzhaft, entschlossen.

Egmont. Ja, wenn's nicht gar zu bunt geht. Diesmal ist sie doch ein wenig aus der Fassung.[27]

Clärchen. Wie so?

Egmont. Sie hat auch ein Bärtchen auf der Oberlippe, und manchmal einen Anfall von Podagra. Eine rechte Amazone!

Clärchen. Eine majestätische Frau! Ich scheute mich, vor sie zu treten.

Egmont. Du bist doch sonst nicht zaghaft. — Es wäre auch nicht Furcht, nur jungfräuliche Scham.

Clärchen (schlägt die Augen nieder, nimmt seine Hand und lehnt sich an ihn).

Egmont. Ich verstehe dich! liebes Mädchen! du darfst die Augen aufschlagen. (Er küßt ihre Augen.)

Clärchen. Laß mich schweigen! Laß mich dich halten. Laß mich dir in die Augen sehen; alles drin finden, Trost und Hoff-

---

[24] ist doch noch eine bessere Unterhaltung für sie, affords her still more entertainment.

[25] Verstellt sie sich? Does she dissemble?

[26] Ich könnte mich in die Welt nicht finden, I could not understand their world.

[27] Diesmal ist sie doch ein wenig aus der Fassung, This time she has been put out a little.

nung und Freude und Kummer. (Sie umarmt ihn und sieht ihn an.) Sag' mir! Sage! ich begreife nicht! bist du Egmont? der Graf Egmont? der große Egmont, der so viel Aufsehn macht, von dem in den Zeitungen steht, an dem die Provinzen hängen?

Egmont. Nein, Clärchen, das bin ich nicht.

Clärchen. Wie?

Egmont. Siehst du, Clärchen! — Laß mich sitzen! — (Er setzt sich, sie kniet vor ihn auf einen Schemel, legt ihre Arme auf seinen Schooß und sieht ihn an.) Jener Egmont ist ein verdrießlicher, steifer, kalter Egmont, der an sich halten, bald dieses bald jenes Gesicht machen muß;[28] geplagt, verkannt, verwickelt ist,[29] wenn ihn die Leute für froh und fröhlich halten; geliebt von einem Volke, das nicht weiß, was es will; geehrt und in die Höhe getragen von einer Menge, mit der nichts anzufangen ist;[30] umgeben von Freunden, denen er sich nicht überlassen darf; beobachtet von Menschen, die ihm auf alle Weise beikommen möchten; arbeitend und sich bemühend, oft ohne Zweck, meist ohne Lohn — o, laß mich schweigen, wie es dem ergeht, wie es dem zu Muthe ist. Aber dieser, Clärchen, der ist ruhig, offen, glücklich, geliebt und gekannt von dem besten Herzen, das auch er ganz kennt und mit voller Liebe und Zutraun an das seine drückt. (Er umarmt sie.) Das ist dein Egmont!

Clärchen. So laß mich sterben! Die Welt hat keine Freuden auf diese![31]

---

[28] ein verdrießlicher, steifer, kalter Egmont, der an sich halten . . . muß, an unpleasant, stiff, and cold Egmont, who must restrain himself.

[29] der geplagt, verkannt, verwickelt ist, who is plagued, misconstrued, entangled.

[30] mit der nichts anzufangen ist, with which one can do nothing.

[31] Die Welt hat keine Freuden auf diese! The world has no joys after this!

Vierter Aufzug.

Erste Scene.

Straße.

Jetter. Zimmermeister.

Jetter. He! pst! he, Nachbar, ein Wort!

Zimmermeister. Geh deines Pfads und sei ruhig.

Jetter. Nur ein Wort. Nichts neues?

Zimmermeister. Nichts, als daß uns von neuem zu reden verboten ist.[1]

Jetter. Wie?

Zimmermeister. Tretet hier ans Haus an. Hütet euch! Der Herzog von Alba[2] hat gleich bei seiner Ankunft einen Befehl ausgehen lassen,[3] dadurch zwei oder drei, die auf der Straße zusammen sprechen, des Hochverraths ohne Untersuchung schuldig erklärt sind.

Jetter. O weh!

Zimmermeister. Bei ewiger Gefangenschaft ist verboten,[4] von Staatssachen zu reden.

Jetter. O unsre Freiheit!

Zimmermeister. Und bei Todesstrafe soll niemand die Handlungen der Regierung mißbilligen.

Jetter. O unsre Köpfe!

Zimmermeister. Und mit großem Versprechen werden

---

[1] Nichts, als daß uns von neuem zu reden verboten ist, Nothing but that we have again been forbidden to talk.

[2] der Herzog von Alba. Vide Note 8, Act III. Scene 1. He arrived August 1567.

[3] einen Befehl ausgehen lassen, sent forth an edict.

[4] Bei ewiger Gefangenschaft ist verboten, it is forbidden under a penalty of perpetual imprisonment.

Väter, Mütter, Kinder, Verwandte, Freunde, Dienstboten eingeladen, was in dem Innersten des Hauses vorgeht, bei dem besonders niedergesetzten Gerichte zu offenbaren.[5]

Jetter. Gehn wir nach Hause.

Zimmermeister. Und den Folgsamen ist versprochen, daß sie weder an Leibe, noch Ehre, noch Vermögen einige Kränkung erdulden sollen.

Jetter. Wie gnädig! War mir's doch gleich weh, wie der Herzog in die Stadt kam. Seit der Zeit ist mir's, als wäre der Himmel mit einem schwarzen Flor überzogen und hinge so tief herunter, daß man sich bücken müsse, um nicht dran zu stoßen.[6]

Zimmermeister. Und wie haben dir seine Soldaten gefallen? Gelt! das ist eine andre Art von Krebsen,[7] als wir sie sonst gewohnt waren.

Jetter. Pfui! Es schnürt einem das Herz ein, wenn man so einen Haufen die Gassen hinab marschiren sieht. Kerzengerad',[8] mit unverwandtem Blick, ein Tritt, so viel ihrer sind. Und wenn sie auf der Schildwache stehen, und du gehst an einem vorbei, ist's, als wenn er dich durch und durch sehen wollte, und sieht so steif und mürrisch aus, daß du auf allen Ecken einen Zuchtmeister zu sehen glaubst.[9] Sie thun mir gar nicht wohl. Unsre Miliz war doch noch ein lustig Volk; sie nahmen sich was heraus, standen mit ausgegrätschten Beinen da,[10] hatten den Hut überm Ohr, lebten und ließen leben; diese Kerle aber sind wie Maschinen, in denen ein Teufel sitzt.

---

[5] bei dem besonders niedergesetzten Gerichte zu offenbaren, to report to the tribunal specially appointed. This tribunal consisted of twelve judges, over which at first the duke himself, and subsequently Juan de Vargas, presided.

[6] daß man sich bücken müsse, um nicht dran zu stoßen, that one had to stoop in order to escape touching it.

[7] Gelt! das ist eine andre Art von Krebsen, I bet you they are a different sort of crabs.

[8] kerzengrad, straight as a poplar.

[9] daß du auf allen Ecken einen Zuchtmeister zu sehen glaubst, that you seem to see a taskmaster at every corner.

[10] standen mit ausgegrätschten Beinen da, stood at ease, lit. with their legs wide apart.

Zimmermeister. Wenn so einer ruft: „Halt!“ und anschlägt,[11] meinst du, man hielte?

Jetter. Ich wäre gleich des Todes.

Zimmermeister. Gehn wir nach Hause.

Jetter. Es wird nicht gut. Adieu.

Soest tritt auf.

Freunde! Genossen!

Zimmermeister. Still! Laßt uns gehen.

Soest. Wißt ihr?

Jetter. Nur zu viel!

Soest. Die Regentin ist weg.[12]

Jetter. Nun gnad' uns Gott!

Zimmermeister. Die hielt uns noch.

Soest. Auf einmal und in der Stille. Sie konnte sich mit dem Herzog nicht vertragen; sie ließ dem Adel melden, sie komme wieder. Niemand glaubt's.

Zimmermeister. Gott verzeih's dem Adel, daß er uns diese neue Geißel über den Hals gelassen hat.[13] Sie hätten es abwenden können. Unsre Privilegien sind hin.

Jetter. Um Gottes willen nichts von Privilegien! Ich wittre den Geruch von einem Executionsmorgen; die Sonne will nicht hervor, die Nebel stinken.

Soest. Oranien ist auch weg.

Zimmermeister. So sind wir denn ganz verlassen!

Soest. Graf Egmont ist noch da.

Jetter. Gott sei Dank! Stärken ihn alle Heiligen, daß er sein Bestes thut; der ist allein was vermögend.

---

[11] anschlägt, aims at you.

[12] Die Regentin ist weg. The regent had written in February 1567 to Philipp, stating she was sure he would never be unjust, and do a thing so prejudicial to the interests of the country, as to transfer to another the powers he had vested in her; and she resigned her post immediately upon the arrival of Aloa, who had taken up his residence at the Culenburg Palace. She did not, however, leave, as stated in the text, until after the arrest of Counts Egmont and Hoorne.

[13] daß er uns diese neue Geißel über den Hals gelassen hat, that they have permitted this new scourge to fall on us.

Vansen tritt auf.

Find' ich endlich ein Paar, die noch nicht untergekrochen sind?[14]

Jetter. Thut uns den Gefallen und geht fürbaß.[15]

Vansen. Ihr seid nicht höflich.

Zimmermeister. Es ist gar keine Zeit zu Complimenten. Juckt euch der Buckel wieder? Seid ihr schon durchgeheilt?[16]

Vansen. Fragt einen Soldaten nach seinen Wunden! Wenn ich auf Schläge was gegeben hätte, wäre sein Tage nichts aus mir geworden.

Jetter. Es kann ernstlicher werden.

Vansen. Ihr spürt von dem Gewitter, das aufsteigt, eine erbärmliche Mattigkeit in den Gliedern, scheint's.

Zimmermeister. Deine Glieder werden sich bald wo anders eine Motion machen,[17] wenn du nicht ruhst.

Vansen. Armselige Mäuse, die gleich verzweifeln, wenn der Hausherr eine neue Katze anschafft![18] Nur ein Bischen anders; aber wir treiben unser Wesen vor wie nach, seid nur ruhig.

Zimmermeister. Du bist ein verwegner Taugenichts.

Vansen. Gevatter Tropf! Laß du den Herzog nur gewähren. Der alte Kater sieht aus, als wenn er Teufel statt Mäuse gefressen hätte und könnte sie nun nicht verdauen.[19] Laßt ihn nur erst; er muß auch essen, trinken, schlafen wie andere Menschen. Es ist mir nicht bange, wenn wir unsere Zeit recht nehmen. Im Anfange geht's rasch; nachher wird er auch finden, daß in der Speisekammer unter den Speckseiten besser leben ist und des Nachts zu ruhen, als auf dem Fruchtboden einzelne Mäuschen zu erlisten.[20] Geht nur, ich kenne die Statthalter.

---

[14] die noch nicht untergekrochen sind, that have not yet crept under, i. e. hidden themselves.

[15] fürbaß, your way.

[16] Seid ihr schon durchgeheilt? Are you already healed thoroughly?

[17] werden sich bald wo anders Motion machen, will soon move somewhere else.

[18] eine neue Katze anschafft, gets a new cat.

[19] und könnte sie nun nicht verdauen, and could not digest them.

[20] als auf dem Fruchtboden einzelne Mäuschen zu erlisten, than to catch in the barn a few mice.

Zimmermeister. Was so einem Menschen alles durchgeht![21] Wenn ich in meinem Leben so etwas gesagt hätte, hielt' ich mich keine Minute für sicher.

Vansen. Seid nur ruhig. Gott im Himmel erfährt nichts von euch Würmern, geschweige[22] der Regent.

Jetter. Lästermaul!

Vansen. Ich weiß andere, denen es besser wäre, sie hätten statt ihres Heldenmuths eine Schneiderader im Leibe.

Zimmermeister. Was wollt ihr damit sagen?

Vansen. Hm! den Grafen mein' ich.

Jetter. Egmont! Was soll der fürchten?

Vansen. Ich bin ein armer Teufel und könnte ein ganzes Jahr leben von dem, was er in einem Abende verliert. Und doch könnt' er mir sein Einkommen eines ganzen Jahrs geben, wenn er meinen Kopf auf eine Viertelstunde hätte.[23]

Jetter. Du denkst dich was rechts. Egmonts Haare sind gescheiter als dein Hirn.

Vansen. Red't ihr! Aber nicht feiner. Die Herren betrügen sich am ersten.[24] Er sollte nicht trauen.

Jetter. Was er schwätzt! So ein Herr!

Vansen. Eben weil er kein Schneider ist.

Jetter. Ungewaschen Maul!

Vansen. Dem wollt' ich eure Courage nur eine Stunde in die Glieder wünschen, daß sie ihm da Unruh machte und ihn so lange neckte und juckte, bis er aus der Stadt müßte.

Jetter. Ihr redet recht unverständig; er ist so sicher wie der Stern am Himmel.

Vansen. Hast du nie einen sich schneuzen gesehn?[25] Weg war er!

---

[21] Was so einem Menschen alles durchgeht! I wonder what such a fellow dare say with impunity.

[22] erfährt nichts von euch Würmern, geschweige, &c. hears nothing of you worms, much less, &c.

[23] wenn er meinen Kopf auf eine Viertelstunde hätte, if he had my head for a quarter of an hour.

[24] betrügen sich am ersten, are soonest deceived.

[25] Hast du nie einen sich schneuzen gesehn? Have you never seen one (i. e. a star) shoot, fall?

Zimmermeister. Wer will ihm denn was thun?

Vansen. Wer will? Willst du's etwa hindern? Willst du einen Aufruhr erregen, wenn sie ihn gefangen nehmen?

Jetter. Ah!

Vansen. Wollt ihr eure Rippen für ihn wagen?

Soest. Eh!

Vansen (sie nachäffend). Ih! Oh! Uh! Verwundert euch durchs ganze Alphabet. So ist's und bleibt's! Gott bewahre ihn!

Jetter. Ich erschrecke über eure Unverschämtheit. So ein edler, rechtschaffener Mann sollte was zu befürchten haben?

Vansen. Der Schelm sitzt überall im Vortheil.[26] Auf dem Armensünder-Stühlchen hat er den Richter zum Narren; auf dem Richterstuhl macht er den Inquisiten mit Lust zum Verbrecher.[27] Ich habe so ein Protocoll abzuschreiben gehabt, wo der Commissarius schwer Lob und Geld vom Hofe erhielt, weil er einen ehrlichen Teufel, an den man wollte,[28] zum Schelmen verhört hatte.

Zimmermeister. Das ist wieder frisch gelogen. Was wollen sie denn heraus verhören, wenn einer unschuldig ist?

Vansen. O Spatzenkopf! Wo nichts heraus zu verhören ist, da verhört man hinein.[29] Ehrlichkeit macht unbesonnen, auch wohl trotzig. Da fragt man erst sachte weg, und der Gefangne ist stolz auf seine Unschuld, wie sie's heißen, und sagt alles gerad' zu, was ein Verständiger verbärge. Dann macht der Inquisitor aus den Antworten wieder Fragen und paßt ja auf, wo irgend ein Widersprüchelchen erscheinen will; da knüpft er seinen Strick an; und läßt sich der dumme Teufel betreten,[30] daß

---

[26] Der Schelm sitzt überall im Vortheil, The rogue is everywhere at an advantage.

[27] Auf dem Armensünder-Stühlchen hat er den Richter zum Narren; auf dem Richterstuhl macht er den Inquisiten mit Lust zum Verbrecher, On the condemned seat, he makes a fool of the judge; in the judge's seat, he takes a delight in making the witness, lit. the examined, a criminal.

[28] an den man wollte, against whom they had a grudge.

[29] Wo nichts heraus zu verhören ist, da verhört man hinein, Where nothing is to come out by cross-examining, one imports it.

[30] und läßt sich der dumme Teufel betreten, and if the fool allows himself to be frightened.

er hier etwas zu viel, dort etwas zu wenig gesagt, oder wohl gar aus Gott weiß was für einer Grille[31] einen Umstand verschwiegen hat, auch wohl irgend an einem Ende sich hat schrecken lassen; dann sind wir auf dem rechten Weg! Und ich versichere euch, mit mehr Sorgfalt suchen die Bettelweiber nicht die Lumpen aus dem Kehricht, als so ein Schelmenfabricant aus kleinen, schiefen, verschobenen, verrückten, verdrückten, geschlossenen, bekannten, geläugneten Anzeigen und Umständen[32] sich endlich einen strohlumpenen Vogelscheu zusammenkünstelt,[33] um wenigstens seinen Inquisiten in effigie hängen zu können. Und Gott mag der arme Teufel danken, wenn er sich noch kann hängen sehen.

Jetter. Der hat eine geläufige Zunge.

Zimmermeister. Mit Fliegen mag das angehen. Die Wespen lachen eures Gespinnstes.[34]

Vansen. Nachdem die Spinnen sind. Seht, der lange Herzog hat euch so ein rein Ansehn von einer Kreuzspinne, nicht einer dickbäuchigen, die sind weniger schlimm, aber so einer langfüßigen, schmalleibigen, die vom Fraße nicht feist wird und recht dünne Fäden zieht, aber desto zähere.

Jetter. Egmont ist Ritter des goldnen Vließes; wer darf Hand an ihn legen? Nur von seines Gleichen kann er gerichtet werden, nur vom gesammten Orden. Dein loses Maul, dein böses Gewissen verführen dich zu solchem Geschwätz.

Vansen. Will ich ihm darum übel? Mir kann's recht sein. Es ist ein trefflicher Herr. Ein Paar meiner guten Freunde, die anderwärts schon wären gehangen worden, hat er mit einem Buckel voll Schläge verabschiedet.[35] Nun geht! Geht! Ich

[31] oder wohl gar aus Gott weiß was für einer Grille, or from some whim or other.

[32] als so ein Schelmenfabricant aus kleinen, schiefen, verschobenen, verrückten, verdrückten, geschlossenen, bekannten, geläugneten Anzeigen und Umständen, than such a rogue-maker from small, crooked, displaced, misplaced, squeezed, concluded, confessed, denied surmises and circumstances.

[33] sich endlich einen strohlumpenen Vogelscheu zusammenkünstelt, patches up at last a straw-stuffed scarecrow.

[34] Wespen lachen eures Gespinnstes, wasps laugh at your web.

[35] hat er mit einem Buckel voll Schläge verabschiedet, he has let off with a beating. Comp. Act II. Scene 2, Note 8.

rath' es euch selbst. Dort seh' ich wieder eine Runde antreten; die sehen nicht aus, als wenn sie so bald Brüderschaft mit uns trinken würden.[36] Wir wollen's abwarten, und nur sachte zusehen. Ich hab' einen Gevatter Schenkwirth; wenn sie von dem gekostet haben, und werden dann nicht zahm, so sind sie ausgepichte Wölfe.

Zweite Scene.

Der Culenburgische Palast.

Wohnung des Herzogs von Alba.

Silva und Gomez begegnen einander.

Silva. Hast du die Befehle des Herzogs ausgerichtet?

Gomez. Pünktlich. Alle täglichen Runden sind beordert,[1] zur bestimmten Zeit an verschiedenen Plätzen einzutreffen, die ich ihnen bezeichnet habe; sie gehen indeß, wie gewöhnlich, durch die Stadt, um Ordnung zu erhalten. Keiner weiß von dem andern; jeder glaubt, der Befehl gehe ihn allein an,[2] und in einem Augenblick kann alsdann der Cordon gezogen, und alle Zugänge zum Palast können besetzt sein.[3] Weißt du die Ursache dieses Befehls?

Silva. Ich bin gewohnt, blindlings zu gehorchen. Und wem gehorcht sich's leichter als dem Herzoge? da bald der Ausgang beweist, daß er recht befohlen hat.

Gomez. Gut! Gut! Auch scheint es mir kein Wunder, daß du so verschlossen und einsylbig wirst wie er, da du immer um ihn

---

[36] als wenn sie so bald Brüderschaft mit uns trinken würden, as if they were going to be so soon our boon companions, lit. were going to drink brotherhood with us.

Second Scene.

The Culenburg Palace, situated on the *Sablon* square, not far from the hill on which the castle of the ancient dukes of Brabant stood; it was pulled down some time after 1570, and a Carmelite church erected on the spot, on the ruins of which is now built a *maison de dètention*.

---

[1] Alle tägliche Runden sind beordert, all the daily rounds have orders.

[2] der Befehl gehe ihn allein an, the order concerns him only.

[3] können besetzt sein, can be occupied.

sein mußt.[4] Mir kommt es fremd vor, da ich den leichteren Italiänischen Dienst gewohnt bin. An Treue und Gehorsam bin ich der alte; aber ich habe mir das Schwätzen und Raisonniren angewöhnt. Ihr schweigt alle und laßt es euch nie wohl sein.[5] Der Herzog gleicht mir einem ehernen Thurm ohne Pforte, wozu die Besatzung Flügel hätte. Neulich hört' ich ihn bei der Tafel von einem frohen, freundlichen Menschen sagen: er sei wie eine schlechte Schenke mit einem ausgesteckten Branntweinzeichen, um Müßiggänger, Bettler und Diebe herein zu locken.[6]

Silva. Und hat er uns nicht schweigend hierher geführt?

Gomez. Dagegen ist nichts zu sagen. Gewiß! Wer Zeuge seiner Klugheit war, wie er die Armee aus Italien hierher brachte, der hat etwas gesehen. Wie er sich durch Freund und Feind, durch die Franzosen, Königlichen und Ketzer, durch die Schweizer und Verbundenen gleichsam durchschmiegte,[7] die strengste Mannszucht hielt,[8] und einen Zug, den man so gefährlich achtete, leicht

---

[4] da du immer um ihn sein mußt, as you have always to be with him.

[5] und laßt es euch nie wohl sein, and are never merry.

[6] er sei wie eine schlechte Schenke mit einem ausgesteckten Branntweinzeichen, um Müßiggänger, Bettler und Diebe herein zu locken, he was like a bad tap, with a toper's sign hung out, to allure idlers, beggars, and thieves.

[7] gleichsam durchschmiegte, squeezed himself through, as it were.

[8] die strengste Mannszucht hielt, kept the strictest discipline. The march alluded to here began soon after April 15, 1567, when Alva had his last audience of Philip at Aranguez. He set out from Carthagena, and landed at Savona. The troops, consisting of about 10,000 men, 1,300 of whom were cavalry, were the choicest Spain could produce, of whom Brantôme remarks that they looked more like captains than soldiers. Alva dispensed with artillery, not wishing to encumber his movements, marched over the Mont Cenis, following Hannibal's route, past Geneva, the citizens of which Protestant canton expected hourly to be attacked, through Lorraine, and crossed the frontiers of the Netherlands on August 8. 'This march,' in the language of Prescott, 'had been accomplished without an untoward accident, and with scarcely a disorderly act on the part of the soldiers. No man's property had been plundered. No peasant's hut had been violated. The most admirable discipline had been maintained, which was all the more conspicuous in an age when the name of soldier was synonymous with marauder.'

und ohne Anstoß zu leiten wußte! — Wir haben was gesehen, was lernen können.

Silva. Auch hier! Ist nicht alles still und ruhig, als wenn kein Aufstand gewesen wäre?

Gomez. Nun, es war auch schon meist still, als wir herkamen.

Silva. In den Provinzen ist es viel ruhiger geworden; und wenn sich noch einer bewegt, so ist es, um zu entfliehen. Aber auch diesem wird er die Wege bald versperren,[9] denk' ich.

Gomez. Nun wird er erst die Gunst des Königs gewinnen.

Silva. Und uns bleibt nichts angelegner,[10] als uns die seinige zu erhalten. Wenn der König hierher kommt, bleibt gewiß der Herzog und jeder, den er empfiehlt, nicht unbelohnt.

Gomez. Glaubst du, daß der König kommt?

Silva. Es werden so viele Anstalten gemacht, daß es höchst wahrscheinlich ist.

Gomez. Mich überreden sie nicht.

Silva. So rede wenigstens nicht davon. Denn wenn des Königs Absicht ja nicht sein sollte, zu kommen, so ist sie's doch wenigstens gewiß, daß man es glauben soll.

Ferdinand, Alba's natürlicher Sohn.[11]

Ist mein Vater noch nicht heraus?

Silva. Wir warten auf ihn.

Ferdinand. Die Fürsten werden bald hier sein.

Gomez. Kommen sie heute?

Ferdinand. Oranien und Egmont.

Gomez (leise zu Silva). Ich begreife etwas.[12]

Silva. So behalt' es für dich.[13]

---

[9] wird er die Wege bald versperren, he will soon bar the road.

[10] bleibt nichts angelegner, nothing is of greater importance.

[11] Alva had both his sons with him, Frederic and Ferdinand of Toledo, for whom he showed an especial liking, and to whom he had entrusted the command of the cavalry during the famous march.

[12] Ich begreife etwas, I have a suspicion.

[13] So behalt' es für dich, Then keep it to yourself.

Herzog von Alba.

(Wie er herein= und hervortritt, treten die andern zurück.)

Gomez!

Gomez (tritt vor). Herr!

Alba. Du hast die Wachen vertheilt und beordert?

Gomez. Aufs genauste. Die täglichen Runden —

Alba. Genug. Du wartest in der Galerie. Silva wird dir den Augenblick sagen, wenn du sie zusammenziehen, die Zugänge nach dem Palast besetzen sollst. Das übrige weißt du.

Gomez. Ja, Herr! (Ab.)

Alba. Silva!

Silva. Hier bin ich.

Alba. Alles was ich von jeher an dir geschätzt habe, Muth, Entschlossenheit, unaufhaltsames Ausführen, das zeige heut.

Silva. Ich danke euch, daß ihr mir Gelegenheit gebt, zu zeigen, daß ich der alte bin.

Alba. Sobald die Fürsten bei mir eingetreten sind, dann eile gleich, Egmonts Geheimschreiber gefangen zu nehmen. Du hast alle Anstalten gemacht, die übrigen, welche bezeichnet sind, zu fahen?[14]

Silva. Vertrau' auf uns. Ihr Schicksal wird sie, wie eine wohlberechnete Sonnenfinsterniß,[15] pünktlich und schrecklich treffen.

Alba. Hast du sie genau beobachten lassen?

Silva. Alle; den Egmont vor andern. Er ist der einzige, der, seit du hier bist, sein Betragen nicht geändert hat. Den ganzen Tag von einem Pferd aufs andere, ladet Gäste, ist immer lustig und unterhaltend bei Tafel, würfelt, schießt und schleicht Nachts zum Liebchen. Die andern haben dagegen eine merkliche

---

[14] die übrigen, welche bezeichnet sind, zu fahen, to take prisoners the remainder who have been designated.

[15] wie eine wohlberechnete Sonnenfinsterniß, like a well-calculated eclipse.

Pause in ihrer Lebensart gemacht; sie bleiben bei sich; vor ihrer Thüre steht's aus,[16] als wenn ein Kranker im Hause wäre.

Alba. Drum rasch! eh sie uns wider Willen genesen.[17]

Silva. Ich stelle sie. Auf deinen Befehl überhäufen wir sie mit dienstfertigen Ehren.[18] Ihnen graut's; politisch geben sie uns einen ängstlichen Dank, fühlen, das räthlichste sei, zu entfliehen. Keiner wagt einen Schritt, sie zaudern, können sich nicht vereinigen; und einzeln etwas Kühnes zu thun, hält sie der Gemeingeist ab. Sie möchten gern sich jedem Verdacht entziehen und machen sich immer verdächtiger. Schon seh' ich mit Freuden deinen ganzen Anschlag ausgeführt.[19]

Alba. Ich freue mich nur über das Geschehene, und auch über das nicht leicht; denn es bleibt stets noch übrig, was uns zu denken und zu sorgen giebt. Das Glück ist eigensinnig, oft das Gemeine, das Nichtswürdige zu adeln und wohlüberlegte Thaten mit einem gemeinen Ausgang zu entehren.[20] Verweile, bis die Fürsten kommen; dann gieb Gomez die Ordre, die Straßen zu besetzen, und eile selbst, Egmonts Schreiber und die übrigen gefangen zu nehmen, die dir bezeichnet sind. Ist es gethan, so komm hierher und meld' es meinem Sohne, daß er mir in den Rath die Nachricht bringe.

Silva. Ich hoffe diesen Abend vor dir stehn zu dürfen.

Alba (geht nach seinem Sohne, der bisher in der Galerie gestanden).

Silva. Ich traue mir es nicht zu sagen; aber meine Hoffnung schwankt. Ich fürchte, es wird nicht werden, wie er denkt. Ich sehe Geister vor mir, die still und sinnend auf schwarzen Schalen das Geschick der Fürsten und vieler Tausende wägen.

---

[16] vor ihrer Thüre steht's aus, before their doors things look.

[17] wider Willen genesen, recover against our will.

[18] überhäufen wir sie mit dienstfertigen Ehren, we heap upon them obliging honours.

[19] seh' ich mit Freuden deinen ganzen Anschlag ausgeführt, I see with much joy your entire plan executed.

[20] und wohlüberlegte Thaten mit einem gemeinen Ausgang zu entehren, and to dishonour well-matured plans by a mean result.

Langsam wankt das Zünglein auf und ab; tief scheinen die Richter zu sinnen; zuletzt sinkt diese Schale, steigt jene, angehaucht vom Eigensinn des Schicksals, und entschieden ist's.[21]

(Ab.)

Alba (mit Ferdinand hervortretend). Wie fandst du die Stadt?

Ferdinand. Es hat sich alles gegeben. Ich ritt, als wie zum Zeitvertreib, Straß' auf Straß' ab. Eure wohlvertheilten Wachen halten die Furcht so angespannt,[22] daß sie sich nicht zu lispeln untersteht. Die Stadt sieht einem Felde ähnlich, wenn das Gewitter von weitem leuchtet; man erblickt keinen Vogel, kein Thier, als das eilend nach einem Schutzorte schlüpft.

Alba. Ist dir nichts weiter begegnet?

Ferdinand. Egmont kam mit einigen auf den Markt geritten; wir grüßten uns; er hatte ein rohes Pferd,[23] das ich ihm loben mußte. „Laßt uns eilen, Pferde zuzureiten,[24] wir werden sie bald brauchen!" rief er mir entgegen. Er werde mich noch heute wiedersehn, sagte er, und komme auf euer Verlangen, mit euch zu rathschlagen.

Alba. Er wird dich wiedersehn.

Ferdinand. Unter allen Rittern, die ich hier kenne, gefällt er mir am besten. Es scheint, wir werden Freunde sein.

Alba. Du bist noch immer zu schnell und wenig behutsam; immer erkenn' ich in dir den Leichtsinn deiner Mutter. Zu mancher gefährlichen Verbindung lud dich der Anschein voreilig ein.[25]

---

[21] Langsam wankt das Zünglein auf und ab; tief scheinen die Richter zu sinnen; zuletzt sinkt diese Schale, steigt jene, angehaucht vom Eigensinn des Schicksals, und entschieden ist's, Slowly the needle moves up and down; the judges seem to deliberate; at last this scale sinks, that one rises, impelled by stubborn fate, and the matter is decided.

[22] Eure wohlvertheilten Wachen halten die Furcht so angespannt, your well-distributed guards have caused such a fear.

[23] er hatte ein rohes Pferd, he had an unbroken horse.

[24] Pferde zuzureiten, to break in horses.

[25] Zu mancher gefährlichen Verbindung lud dich der Anschein voreilig ein, Into many a dangerous companionship, appearances have drawn thee inconsiderately.

Ferdinand. Euer Wille findet mich bildsam.

Alba. Ich vergebe deinem jungen Blute dies leichtsinnige Wohlwollen, diese unachtsame Fröhlichkeit.[26] Nur vergiß nicht, zu welchem Werke ich gesandt bin, und welchen Theil ich dir daran geben möchte.

Ferdinand. Erinnert mich, und schont mich nicht, wo ihr es nöthig haltet.

Alba (nach einer Pause). Mein Sohn!

Ferdinand. Mein Vater!

Alba. Die Fürsten kommen bald, Oranien und Egmont kommen. Es ist nicht Mißtrauen, daß ich dir erst jetzt entdecke, was geschehen soll. Sie werden nicht wieder von hinnen gehn.

Ferdinand. Was sinnst du?

Alba. Es ist beschlossen, sie festzuhalten. — Du erstaunst! Was du zu thun hast, höre; die Ursachen sollst du wissen, wenn es geschehen ist. Jetzt bleibt keine Zeit, sie auszulegen.[27] Mit dir allein wünscht' ich das Größte, das Geheimste zu besprechen; ein starkes Band hält uns zusammengefesselt; du bist mir werth und lieb; auf dich möcht' ich alles häufen. Nicht die Gewohnheit zu gehorchen allein möcht' ich dir einprägen; auch den Sinn auszudrücken, zu befehlen, auszuführen, wünscht' ich in dir fortzupflanzen;[28] dir ein großes Erbtheil, dem Könige den brauchbarsten Diener zu hinterlassen; dich mit dem besten, was ich habe, auszustatten, daß du dich nicht schämen dürfest, unter deine Brüder zu treten.

Ferdinand. Was werd' ich dir nicht für diese Liebe schuldig, die du mir allein zuwendest, indem ein ganzes Reich vor dir zittert!

Alba. Nun höre, was zu thun ist. Sobald die Fürsten

---

[26] leichtsinnige Wohlwollen, diese unachtsame Fröhlichkeit, giddy benevolence, this heedless merriment, merry humour.

[27] sie auszulegen, to explain them.

[28] Nicht die Gewohnheit zu gehorchen allein möcht' ich dir einprägen; auch den Sinn auszudrücken, zu befehlen, auszuführen, wünscht' ich in dir fortzupflanzen, Not only the habit of obedience, I should wish to impress upon thee, I should wish to continue in thee also the power to express thyself, to command, to execute.

eingetreten sind, wird jeder Zugang zum Palaste besetzt. Dazu hat Gomez die Ordre. Silva wird eilen, Egmonts Schreiber mit den Verdächtigsten gefangen zu nehmen. Du hältst die Wache am Thore und in den Höfen in Ordnung.[29] Vor allen Dingen besetze diese Zimmer hier neben mit den sichersten Leuten; dann warte auf der Galerie, bis Silva wiederkommt, und bringe mir irgend ein unbedeutend Blatt herein, zum Zeichen, daß sein Auftrag ausgerichtet ist. Dann bleib im Vorsaale, bis Oranien weggeht; folg' ihm; ich halte Egmont hier, als ob ich ihm noch was zu sagen hätte. Am Ende der Galerie fordre Oraniens Degen, rufe die Wache an, verwahre schnell den gefährlichsten Mann;[30] und ich fasse Egmont hier.

Ferdinand. Ich gehorche, mein Vater. Zum erstenmal mit schwerem Herzen und mit Sorge.

Alba. Ich verzeihe dir's; es ist der erste große Tag, den du erlebst.

Silva tritt herein.

Ein Bote von Antwerpen. Hier ist Oraniens Brief! Er kommt nicht.

Alba. Sagt' es der Bote?

Silva. Nein, mir sagt's das Herz.

Alba. Aus dir spricht mein böser Genius. (Nachdem er den Brief gelesen, winkt er beiden, und sie ziehen sich in die Galerie zurück. Er bleibt allein auf dem Vordertheile.) Er kommt nicht! Bis auf den letzten Augenblick verschiebt er,[31] sich zu erklären. Er wagt es, nicht zu kommen! So war denn diesmal wider Vermuthen der Kluge klug genug, nicht klug zu sein! — Es rückt die Uhr![32] Noch einen kleinen Weg des Seigers,[33] und ein großes Werk ist gethan oder versäumt, un-

---

[29] du hältst die Wache . . . in Ordnung, you keep the watch in order.

[30] verwahre schnell den gefährlichsten Mann, quickly secure the most dangerous man.

[31] verschiebt er, he delays.

[32] Es rückt die Uhr! Time passes.

[33] Seiger, commonly Zeiger, lit. pointer; the hand.

wiederbringlich versäumt; denn es ist weder nachzuholen noch zu verheimlichen. Längst hatt' ich alles reiflich abgewogen, und mir auch diesen Fall gedacht, mir festgesetzt, was auch in diesem Falle zu thun sei; und jetzt, da es zu thun ist, wehr' ich mir kaum, daß nicht das Für und Wider mir aufs neue durch die Seele schwankt.[34] — Ist's räthlich, die andern zu fangen, wenn Er mir entgeht? — Schieb' ich es auf, und lass' Egmont mit den Seinigen, mit so vielen entschlüpfen, die nun, vielleicht nur heute noch, in meinen Händen sind? So zwingt dich das Geschick denn auch, du Unbezwinglicher?[35] Wie lang' gedacht! Wie wohl bereitet! Wie groß, wie schön der Plan! Wie nah' die Hoffnung ihrem Ziele! Und nun im Augenblick des Entscheidens bist du zwischen zwei Uebel gestellt; wie in einen Loostopf greifst du[36] in die dunkle Zukunft; was du fassest, ist noch zugerollt, dir unbewußt, sei's Treffer oder Fehler![37] (Er wird aufmerksam, wie einer, der etwas hört, und tritt ans Fenster.) Er ist es! — Egmont! Trug dich dein Pferd so leicht herein, und scheute vor dem Blutgeruche nicht,[38] und vor dem Geiste mit dem blanken Schwert, der an der Pforte dich empfängt? — Steig ab! — So bist du mit dem einen Fuß im Grab! und so mit beiden! — Ja, streichl' es nur, und klopfe für seinen muthigen Dienst zum letztenmale den Nacken ihm — Und mir bleibt keine Wahl. In der Verblendung,[39] wie hier Egmont naht, kann er dir nicht zum zweitenmal sich liefern! — Hört!

Ferdinand und Silva (treten eilig herbei).

Ihr thut, was ich befahl; ich ändre meinen Willen nicht. Ich halte, wie es gehn will, Egmont auf, bis du mir von Silva die

---

[34] aufs neue durch die Seele schwankt, again makes my heart doubtful.

[35] So zwingt dich das Geschick denn auch, du Unbezwinglicher? Fate conquers then even thee, thou unconquerable?

[36] wie in einen Loostopf greifst du, [blindly] thou seizest the dim future as [thou dost] the lottery-urn.

[37] Treffer oder Fehler, prizes or blanks.

[38] scheute vor dem Blutgeruche nicht, did not start back from the smell of blood.

[39] Verblendung, blindness.

Nachricht gebracht hast. Dann bleib in der Nähe. Auch dir raubt das Geschick das große Verdienst, des Königs größten Feind mit eigener Hand gefangen zu haben. (Zu Silva.) Eile! (Zu Ferdinand.) Geh ihm entgegen. (Alba bleibt einige Augenblicke allein und geht schweigend auf und ab.)

Egmont tritt auf.

Ich komme, die Befehle des Königs zu vernehmen, zu hören, welchen Dienst er von unserer Treue verlangt, die ihm ewig ergeben bleibt.

Alba. Er wünscht vor allen Dingen euern Rath zu hören.

Egmont. Ueber welchen Gegenstand? Kommt Oranien auch? Ich vermuthete ihn hier.

Alba. Mir thut es leid, daß er uns eben in dieser wichtigen Stunde fehlt. Euern Rath, eure Meinung wünscht der König, wie diese Staaten wieder zu befriedigen. Ja, er hofft ihr werdet kräftig mitwirken, diese Unruhen zu stillen und die Ordnung der Provinzen völlig und dauerhaft zu gründen.

Egmont. Ihr könnt besser wissen als ich, daß schon alles genug beruhigt ist, ja, noch mehr beruhigt war,[40] eh' die Erscheinung der neuen Soldaten wieder mit Furcht und Sorge die Gemüther bewegte.

Alba. Ihr scheint andeuten zu wollen, das räthlichste sei gewesen, wenn der König mich gar nicht in den Fall gesetzt hätte,[41] euch zu fragen.

Egmont. Verzeiht! Ob der König das Heer hätte schicken sollen, ob nicht vielmehr die Macht seiner majestätischen Gegenwart allein stärker gewirkt hätte, ist meine Sache nicht zu beurtheilen. Das Heer ist da, Er nicht. Wir aber müßten sehr undankbar, sehr vergessen sein, wenn wir uns nicht erinnerten, was wir der Regentin schuldig sind. Bekennen wir! Sie brachte durch ihr so kluges als tapferes Betragen die Aufrührer mit

---

[40] noch mehr beruhigt war, was even still more quiet.

[41] mich gar nicht in den Fall gesetzt hätte, had not given me occasion.

Gewalt und Ansehn, mit Ueberredung und List zur Ruhe, und führte zum Erstaunen der Welt ein rebellisches Volk in wenigen Monaten zu seiner Pflicht zurück.[42]

Alba. Ich läugne es nicht. Der Tumult ist gestillt, und jeder scheint in die Grenzen des Gehorsams zurückgebannt. Aber hängt es nicht von eines jeden Willkür ab,[43] sie zu verlassen? Wer will das Volk hindern, loszubrechen? Wo ist die Macht, sie abzuhalten? Wer bürgt uns, daß sie sich ferner treu und unterthänig zeigen werden? Ihr guter Wille ist alles Pfand,[44] das wir haben.

Egmont. Und ist der gute Wille eines Volks nicht das sicherste, das edelste Pfand? Bei Gott! Wann darf sich ein König sicherer halten, als wenn sie alle für Einen, Einer für alle stehn? Sicherer gegen innere und äußere Feinde?

Alba. Wir werden uns doch nicht überreden sollen, daß es jetzt hier so steht?

Egmont. Der König schreibe einen General-Pardon aus, er beruhige die Gemüther; und bald wird man sehen, wie Treue und Liebe mit dem Zutrauen wieder zurückkehrt.

Alba. Und jeder, der die Majestät des Königs, der das Heiligthum der Religion geschändet, ginge frei und ledig hin und wieder![45] lebte den andern zum bereiten Beispiel, daß ungeheure Verbrechen straflos sind!

Egmont. Und ist ein Verbrechen des Unsinns,[46] der Trunkenheit nicht eher zu entschuldigen, als grausam zu bestrafen?

---

[42] Sie brachte durch ihr so kluges als tapferes Betragen die Aufrührer mit Gewalt und Ansehn, mit Ueberredung und List zur Ruhe, und führte zum Erstaunen der Welt ein rebellisches Volk in wenigen Monaten zu seiner Pflicht zurück, She quieted the rebels by her prudent and bold behaviour, by force and respect, by conviction and artfulness, and, to the astonishment of the world, brought back in a few months a rebellious people to their allegiance.

[43] hängt es nicht von eines jeden Willkür ab? does it not depend on everyone's will?

[44] ist alles Pfand, is the only pledge.

[45] ginge frei und ledig hin und wieder, should come and go free and unhindered.

[46] ein Verbrechen des Unsinns, a crime of madness.

Besonders wo so sichre Hoffnung, wo Gewißheit ist, daß die Uebel nicht wiederkehren werden? Waren Könige darum nicht sicherer? Werden sie nicht von Welt und Nachwelt gepriesen, die eine Beleidigung ihrer Würde vergeben,[47] bedauern, verachten konnten? Werden sie nicht eben deßwegen Gott gleich gehalten, der viel zu groß ist, als daß an ihn jede Lästerung reichen sollte?[48]

Alba. Und eben darum soll der König für die Würde Gottes und der Religion, wir sollen für das Ansehn des Königs streiten. Was der Obere abzulehnen verschmäht, ist unsere Pflicht zu rächen. Ungestraft soll, wenn ich rathe, kein Schuldiger sich freuen.

Egmont. Glaubst du, daß du sie alle erreichen wirst? Hört man nicht täglich, daß die Furcht sie hie- und dahin, sie aus dem Lande treibt? Die Reichsten werden ihre Güter, sich, ihre Kinder und Freunde flüchten;[49] der Arme wird seine nützlichen Hände dem Nachbar zubringen.

Alba. Sie werden, wenn man sie nicht verhindern kann. Darum verlangt der König Rath und That[50] von jedem Fürsten, Ernst von jedem Statthalter; nicht nur Erzählung, wie es ist, was werden könnte, wenn man alles gehen ließe, wie's geht. Einem großen Uebel zusehen, sich mit Hoffnung schmeicheln, der Zeit vertrauen, etwa einmal drein schlagen, wie im Fastnachtsspiel,[51] daß es klatscht und man doch etwas zu thun scheint, wenn man nichts thun möchte, heißt das nicht, sich verdächtig machen, als sehe man dem Aufruhr mit Vergnügen zu, den man nicht erregen, wohl aber hegen möchte?[52]

Egmont (im Begriff aufzufahren, nimmt sich zusammen

---

[47] die eine Beleidigung ihrer Würde vergeben, who forgive that their dignity has been offended.

[48] als daß an ihn jede Lästerung reichen sollte, than that every blasphemy should reach him.

[49] werden flüchten, will save.

[50] Rath und That, counsel and action.

[51] wie im Fastnachtsspiel, as at a carnival.

[52] den man nicht erregen, wohl aber hegen möchte, which one would not like to excite, but still to keep up.

und spricht nach einer kleinen Pause gesetzt). Nicht jede Absicht ist offenbar, und manches Mannes Absicht ist zu mißdeuten. Muß man doch auch von allen Seiten hören: es sei des Königs Absicht weniger, die Provinzen nach einförmigen und klaren Gesetzen zu regieren, die Majestät der Religion zu sichern und einen allgemeinen Frieden seinem Volke zu geben, als vielmehr sie unbedingt zu unterjochen,[53] sie ihrer alten Rechte zu berauben, sich Meister von ihren Besitzthümern zu machen, die schönen Rechte des Adels einzuschränken, um derentwillen[54] der Edle allein ihm dienen, ihm Leib und Leben widmen mag. Die Religion, sagt man, sei nur ein prächtiger Teppich, hinter dem man jeden gefährlichen Anschlag nur desto leichter ausdenkt.[55] Das Volk liegt auf den Knieen, betet die heiligen gewirkten Zeichen an, und hinten lauscht der Vogelsteller, der sie berücken will.[56]

Alba. Das muß ich von dir hören?

Egmont. Nicht meine Gesinnungen! Nur was bald hier, bald da, von Großen und von Kleinen, Klugen und Thoren gesprochen, laut verbreitet wird. Die Niederländer fürchten ein doppeltes Joch, und wer bürgt ihnen für ihre Freiheit?

Alba. Freiheit? Ein schönes Wort, wer's recht verstände. Was wollen sie für Freiheit? Was ist des Freiesten Freiheit? — Recht zu thun! — Und daran wird sie der König nicht hindern. Nein! nein! sie glauben sich nicht frei, wenn sie sich nicht selbst und andern schaden können. Wäre es nicht besser, abzudanken,[57] als ein solches Volk zu regieren? Wenn auswärtige Feinde drängen, an die kein Bürger denkt, der mit dem nächsten nur beschäftigt ist,[58] und der König verlangt Beistand, dann werden sie uneins[59] unter sich, und verschwören sich gleichsam mit

---

[53] sie unbedingt zu unterjochen, unconditionally to enslave them.

[54] um derentwillen, on whose account, for which.

[55] nur desto leichter ausdenkt, matures all the more easily.

[56] der Vogelsteller, der sie berücken will, the bird-catcher, who wants to ensare them.

[57] abzudanken, to abdicate.

[58] der mit dem nächsten nur beschäftigt ist, only troubling himself about what lies close at hand.

[59] werden sie uneins, they disagree.

ihren Feinden. Weit besser ist's, sie einzuengen,[60] daß man sie wie Kinder halten, wie Kinder zu ihrem Besten leiten kann. Glaube nur, ein Volk wird nicht alt, nicht klug; ein Volk bleibt immer kindisch.

Egmont. Wie selten kommt ein König zu Verstand! Und sollen sich viele nicht lieber vielen vertrauen als Einem? und nicht einmal dem Einen, sondern den Wenigen des Einen,[61] dem Volke, das an den Blicken seines Herrn altert. Das hat wohl allein das Recht, klug zu werden.

Alba. Vielleicht eben darum, weil es sich nicht selbst überlassen ist.

Egmont. Und darum niemand gern sich selbst überlassen möchte. Man thue, was man will; ich habe auf deine Frage geantwortet und wiederhole: Es geht nicht! Es kann nicht gehen! Ich kenne meine Landsleute. Es sind Männer, werth Gottes Boden zu betreten; ein jeder rund für sich, ein kleiner König, fest, rührig, fähig, treu,[62] an alten Sitten hangend. Schwer ist's, ihr Zutrauen zu verdienen; leicht, zu erhalten. Starr und fest! Zu drücken sind sie; nicht zu unterdrücken.[63]

Alba (der sich indeß einigemal umgesehen hat). Solltest du das alles in des Königs Gegenwart wiederholen?

Egmont. Desto schlimmer, wenn mich seine Gegenwart abschreckte! Desto besser für ihn, für sein Volk, wenn er mir Muth machte, wenn er mir Zutrauen einflößte, noch weit mehr zu sagen.

Alba. Was nützlich ist, kann ich hören, wie er.

Egmont. Ich würde ihm sagen: Leicht kann der Hirt eine ganze Heerde Schafe vor sich hintreiben, der Stier zieht seinen Pflug ohne Widerstand; aber dem edeln Pferde, das du reiten willst, mußt du seine Gedanken ablernen,[64] du mußt nichts Un-

---

[60] sie einzuengen, to keep them down.

[61] den Wenigen des Einen, to the few of the one.

[62] fest, rührig, fähig, treu, firm, industrious, capable, faithful.

[63] Zu drücken sind sie; nicht zu unterdrücken, They may be pressed, but not oppressed.

[64] mußt du seine Gedanken ablernen, you must learn his thoughts.

kluges, nichts unklug[65] von ihm verlangen. Darum wünscht der Bürger seine alte Verfassung zu behalten, von seinen Landsleuten regiert zu sein, weil er weiß, wie er geführt wird, weil er von ihnen Uneigennutz,[66] Theilnehmung an seinem Schicksal hoffen kann.

Alba. Und sollte der Regent nicht Macht haben, dieses alte Herkommen[67] zu verändern? und sollte nicht eben dies sein schönstes Vorrecht sein? Was ist bleibend auf dieser Welt? und sollte eine Staatseinrichtung[68] bleiben können? Muß nicht in einer Zeitfolge jedes Verhältniß sich verändern und eben darum eine alte Verfassung die Ursache von tausend Uebeln werden, weil sie den gegenwärtigen Zustand des Volkes nicht umfaßt?[69] Ich fürchte, diese alten Rechte sind darum so angenehm, weil sie Schlupfwinkel bilden, in welchen der Kluge, der Mächtige, zum Schaden des Volks, zum Schaden des Ganzen, sich verbergen oder durchschleichen kann.[70]

Egmont. Und diese willkürlichen Veränderungen, diese unbeschränkten Eingriffe der höchsten Gewalt, sind sie nicht Vorboten, daß Einer[71] thun will, was Tausende nicht thun sollen? Er will sich allein frei machen, um jeden seiner Wünsche befriedigen, jeden seiner Gedanken ausführen zu können. Und wenn wir uns ihm, einem guten weisen Könige, ganz vertrauten, sagt er uns für seine Nachkommen gut?[72] daß keiner ohne Rücksicht, ohne Schonung regieren werde? Wer rettet uns alsdann von völliger Willkür, wenn er uns seine Diener, seine Nächsten sendet, die ohne Kenntniß des Landes und seiner Bedürfnisse nach Be-

---

[65] nichts Unkluges, nichts unklug, nothing foolish, nothing foolishly.

[66] Uneigennutz, disinterestedness.

[67] alte Herkommen, old custom.

[68] Staatseinrichtung, constitution.

[69] nicht umfaßt, does not comprehend, is not equal to.

[70] sich verbergen oder durchschleichen kann, may hide or creep through.

[71] Eingriffe der höchsten Gewalt, sind sie nicht Vorboten, daß Einer, &c., encroachments of the supreme power, do they not forebode that one, &c.?

[72] sagt er uns für seine Nachkommen gut? does he guarantee for his descendants?

lieben schalten und walten, keinen Widerstand finden und sich von jeder Verantwortung frei wissen.[73]

Alba (der sich indeß wieder umgesehen hat). Es ist nichts natürlicher, als daß ein König durch sich zu herrschen gedenkt und denen seine Befehle am liebsten aufträgt, die ihn am besten verstehen, verstehen wollen, die seinen Willen unbedingt ausrichten.

Egmont. Und eben so natürlich ist's, daß der Bürger von dem regiert sein will, der mit ihm geboren und erzogen ist, der gleichen Begriff mit ihm von Recht und Unrecht gefaßt hat, den er als seinen Bruder ansehen kann.

Alba. Und doch hat der Adel mit diesen seinen Brüdern sehr ungleich getheilt.[74]

Egmont. Das ist vor Jahrhunderten geschehen und wird jetzt ohne Neid geduldet. Würden aber neue Menschen ohne Noth gesendet, die sich zum zweitenmale auf Unkosten der Nation bereichern wollten, sähe man sich einer strengen, kühnen, unbedingten Habsucht ausgesetzt,[75] das würde eine Gährung machen, die sich nicht leicht in sich selbst auflöste.

Alba. Du sagst mir, was ich nicht hören sollte; auch ich bin fremd.

Egmont. Daß ich dir's sage, zeigt dir, daß ich dich nicht meine.

Alba. Und auch so wünscht' ich es nicht von dir zu hören. Der König sandte mich mit Hoffnung, daß ich hier den Beistand des Adels finden würde. Der König will seinen Willen. Der König hat nach tiefer Ueberlegung gesehen, was dem Volke frommt;[76] es kann nicht bleiben und gehen wie bisher. Des Königs Absicht ist, sie selbst zu ihrem eignen Besten einzuschränken, ihr eigenes Heil, wenn's sein muß, ihnen aufzudringen,[77] die

[73] und sich von jeder Verantwortung frei wissen, and know themselves to be free of all control, of all responsibility.

[74] sehr ungleich getheilt, shared very unequally.

[75] sähe man sich einer strengen, kühnen, unbedingten Habsucht ausgesetzt, were one exposed to a severe, bold, unscrupulous, absolute, greed.

[76] frommt, is beneficial.

[77] ihnen aufzudringen, to force upon them.

schädlichen Bürger aufzuopfern, damit die übrigen Ruhe finden, des Glücks einer weisen Regierung genießen können. Dies ist sein Entschluß; diesen dem Adel kund zu machen, habe ich Befehl; und Rath verlang' ich in seinem Namen, wie es zu thun sei, nicht was: denn das hat Er beschlossen.

Egmont. Leider rechtfertigen deine Worte[78] die Furcht des Volks, die allgemeine Furcht! So hat er denn beschlossen, was kein Fürst beschließen sollte. Die Kraft seines Volks, ihr Gemüth, den Begriff, den sie von sich selbst haben, will er schwächen, niederdrücken, zerstören, um sie bequem regieren zu können. Er will den innern Kern ihrer Eigenheit verderben;[79] gewiß in der Absicht, sie glücklicher zu machen. Er will sie vernichten, damit sie Etwas werden, ein ander Etwas. O, wenn seine Absicht gut ist, so wird sie mißgeleitet! Nicht dem Könige widersetzt man sich; man stellt sich nur dem Könige entgegen, der einen falschen Weg zu wandeln die ersten unglücklichen Schritte macht.[80]

Alba. Wie du gesinnt bist, scheint es ein vergeblicher Versuch, uns vereinigen zu wollen.[81] Du denkst gering vom Könige und verächtlich von seinen Räthen, wenn du zweifelst, das alles sei nicht schon gedacht, geprüft, gewogen worden. Ich habe keinen Auftrag, jedes Für und Wider noch einmal durchzugehen.[82] Gehorsam fordre ich von dem Volke — und von Euch, ihr Ersten, Edelsten, Rath und That, als Bürgen dieser unbedingten Pflicht.[83]

Egmont. Fordre unsre Häupter, so ist es auf einmal gethan. Ob sich der Nacken diesem Joche biegen, ob er sich vor

---

[78] Leider rechtfertigen deine Worte, alas! your words justify.

[79] Er will den innern Kern ihrer Eigenheit verderben, he wants to ruin the kernel (core) of their individuality.

[80] Nicht dem Könige widersetzt man sich; man stellt sich nur dem Könige entgegen, der einen falschen Weg zu wandeln die ersten unglücklichen Schritte macht, One does not rebel against the king; one merely opposes *that* king who has taken the first unhappy steps in a wrong direction.

[81] uns vereinigen zu wollen, to try to unite us.

[82] durchzugehen, to examine.

[83] als Bürgen dieser unbedingten Pflicht, as pledges of this unconditional duty.

dem Beile ducken soll,[84] kann einer edeln Seele gleich sein. Umsonst hab' ich so viel gesprochen; die Luft hab' ich erschüttert, weiter nichts gewonnen.

Ferdinand kommt.

Verzeiht, daß ich euer Gespräch unterbreche. Hier ist ein Brief, dessen Ueberbringer die Antwort dringend macht.

Alba. Erlaubt mir, daß ich sehe, was er enthält. (Tritt an die Seite.)

Ferdinand (zu Egmont). Es ist ein schönes Pferd, das eure Leute gebracht haben, euch abzuholen.

Egmont. Es ist nicht das schlimmste. Ich hab' es schon eine Weile; ich denk' es wegzugeben. Wenn es euch gefällt, so werden wir vielleicht des Handels einig.[85]

Ferdinand. Gut, wir wollen sehn.

Alba (winkt seinem Sohne, der sich in den Grund zurückziehet).

Egmont. Lebt wohl! entlaßt mich: denn ich wüßte bei Gott! nicht mehr zu sagen.

Alba. Glücklich hat dich der Zufall verhindert, deinen Sinn noch weiter zu verrathen. Unvorsichtig entwickelst du die Falten deines Herzens[86] und klagst dich selbst weit strenger an, als ein Widersacher gehässig thun könnte.[87]

Egmont. Dieser Vorwurf rührt mich nicht; ich kenne mich selbst genug und weiß, wie ich dem König angehöre; weit mehr als viele, die in seinem Dienst sich selber dienen. Ungern scheid' ich aus diesem Streite, ohne ihn beigelegt zu sehen,[88] und wünsche nur, daß uns der Dienst des Herrn, das Wohl des Landes bald vereinigen möge. Es wirkt vielleicht ein wieder-

---

[84] ob er sich vor dem Beile ducken soll, whether it is to bow down before the axe.

[85] so werden wir vielleicht des Handels einig, we may perchance agree about the bargain.

[86] Unvorsichtig entwickelst du die Falten deines Herzens, carelessly you unfold your heart.

[87] als ein Widersacher gehässig thun könnte, than an enemy could have done in his hatred.

[88] ohne ihn beigelegt zu seh without seeing it adjusted.

holtes Gespräch,[89] die Gegenwart der übrigen Fürsten, die heute fehlen, in einem glücklichern Augenblick, was heut' unmöglich scheint. Mit dieser Hoffnung entfern' ich mich.

Alba (der zugleich seinem Sohn Ferdinand ein Zeichen giebt). Halt, Egmont! — Deinen Degen! — (Die Mittelthür öffnet sich: man sieht die Galerie mit Wache besetzt, die unbeweglich bleibt.)

Egmont (der staunend eine Weile geschwiegen). Dies war die Absicht? Dazu hast du mich berufen? (Nach dem Degen greifend, als wenn er sich vertheidigen wollte.) Bin ich denn wehrlos?

Alba. Der König befiehlt's, du bist mein Gefangener. (Zugleich treten von beiden Seiten Gewaffnete herein.)

Egmont (nach einer Stille). Der König? — Oranien! Oranien! (Nach einer Pause, seinen Degen hingebend.) So nimm ihn! Er hat weit öfter des Königs Sache vertheidigt[90] als diese Brust beschützt. (Er geht durch die Mittelthür ab: die Gewaffneten, die im Zimmer sind, folgen ihm; ingleichen Alba's Sohn. Alba bleibt stehen. Der Vorhang fällt.)

---

[89] Es wirkt vielleicht ein wiederholtes Gespräch, Maybe that a repeated conversation will effect.

[90] weit öfter des Königs Sache vertheidigt, far oftener defended the king's cause.

Fünfter Aufzug.

Erste Scene.

Straße.

Dämmerung.[1]

Clärchen. Brackenburg. Bürger.

Brackenburg. Liebchen, um Gottes willen, was nimmst du vor?[2]

Clärchen. Komm mit, Brackenburg! Du mußt die Menschen nicht kennen;[3] wir befreien ihn gewiß. Denn was gleicht ihrer Liebe zu ihm? Jeder fühlt, ich schwör' es, in sich die brennende Begier, ihn zu retten, die Gefahr von einem kostbaren Leben abzuwenden und dem Freiesten die Freiheit wiederzugeben. Komm! es fehlt nur an der Stimme,[4] die sie zusammenruft. In ihrer Seele lebt noch ganz frisch, was sie ihm schuldig sind! und daß sein mächtiger Arm allein von ihnen das Verderben abhält, wissen sie. Um seinet- und ihretwillen[5] müssen sie alles wagen. Und was wagen wir? Zum höchsten unser Leben, das zu erhalten nicht der Mühe werth ist, wenn er umkommt.

Brackenburg. Unglückliche! du siehst nicht die Gewalt, die uns mit ehernen Banden gefesselt hat.

Clärchen. Sie scheint mir nicht unüberwindlich. Laß uns nicht lang' vergebliche Worte wechseln. Hier kommen von

---

[1] Dämmerung, dusk.

[2] was nimmst du vor? what is your intention.

[3] Du mußt die Menschen nicht kennen, you cannot know men.

[4] es fehlt nur an der Stimme, the voice only is wanting.

[5] Um seinet- und ihretwillen, for his and their sake.

den alten, redlichen, wackern Männern! Hört, Freunde! Nachbarn, hört! — Sagt, wie ist es mit Egmont?

Zimmermeister. Was will das Kind? Laß sie schweigen!

Clärchen. Tretet näher, daß wir sachte reden, bis wir einig sind und stärker. Wir dürfen nicht einen Augenblick versäumen! Die freche Tyrannei, die es wagt, ihn zu fesseln, zuckt schon den Dolch,[6] ihn zu ermorden. O Freunde! mit jedem Schritt der Dämmerung werd' ich ängstlicher. Ich fürchte diese Nacht. Kommt! wir wollen uns theilen; mit schnellem Lauf von Quartier zu Quartier rufen wir die Bürger heraus. Ein jeder greife zu seinen alten Waffen. Auf dem Markte treffen wir uns wieder, und unser Strom reißt einen jeden mit sich fort. Die Feinde sehen sich umringt und überschwemmt und sind erdrückt. Was kann uns eine Hand voll Knechte widerstehen? Und Er in unsrer Mitte kehrt zurück, sieht sich befreit und kann uns einmal danken, uns, die wir ihm so tief verschuldet worden.[7] Er sieht vielleicht — gewiß, er sieht das Morgenroth am freien Himmel wieder.

Zimmermeister. Wie ist dir, Mädchen?

Clärchen. Könnt ihr mich mißverstehn? Vom Grafen sprech' ich! Ich spreche von Egmont.

Jetter. Nennt den Namen nicht! Er ist tödtlich.

Clärchen. Den Namen nicht! Wie? Nicht diesen Namen? Wer nennt ihn nicht bei jeder Gelegenheit? Wo steht er nicht geschrieben? In diesen Sternen hab' ich oft mit allen seinen Lettern ihn gelesen. Nicht nennen? Was soll das? Freunde! Gute, theure Nachbarn, ihr träumt; besinnt euch. Seht mich nicht so starr und ängstlich an![8] Blickt nicht schüchtern hie und da bei Seite. Ich ruf' euch ja nur zu, was jeder wünscht. Ist meine Stimme nicht eures Herzens eigene Stimme? Wer würfe sich in dieser bangen Nacht, eh' er sein

---

[6] zuckt schon den Dolch, has already lifted the dagger.

[7] die wir ihm so tief verschuldet worden, who are so deeply in his debt.

[8] Seht mich nicht so starr und ängstlich an! Gaze not upon me so anxiously.

unruhvolles Bette besteigt, nicht auf die Kniee, ihn mit ernstlichem Gebet vom Himmel zu erringen?[9] Fragt euch einander! frage jeder sich selbst! und wer spricht mir nicht nach: „Egmonts Freiheit oder den Tod!"

Jetter. Gott bewahr' uns! Da giebt's ein Unglück.

Clärchen. Bleibt! Bleibt, und drückt euch nicht vor seinem Namen weg, dem ihr euch sonst so froh entgegen drängtet! — Wenn der Ruf ihn ankündigte, wenn es hieß: „Egmont kommt! Er kommt von Gent!" da hielten die Bewohner der Straßen sich glücklich, durch die er reiten mußte. Und wenn ihr seine Pferde schallen hörtet, warf jeder seine Arbeit hin, und über die bekümmerten Gesichter, die ihr durchs Fenster stecktet, fuhr wie ein Sonnenstrahl von seinem Angesichte ein Blick der Freude und Hoffnung.[10] Da hobt ihr eure Kinder auf der Thürschwelle in die Höhe und deutetet ihnen: „Sieh, das ist Egmont, der größte da! Er ist's! Er ist's, von dem ihr bessere Zeiten, als eure armen Väter lebten, einst zu erwarten habt." Laßt eure Kinder nicht dereinst euch fragen: „Wo ist er hin? Wo sind die Zeiten hin, die ihr verspracht?" — Und so wechseln wir Worte! sind müßig,[11] verrathen ihn.

Soest. Schämt euch, Brackenburg. Laßt sie nicht gewähren! Steuert dem Unheil![12]

Brackenburg. Liebes Clärchen! wir wollen gehen! Was wird die Mutter sagen? Vielleicht —

Clärchen. Meinst du, ich sei ein Kind, oder wahnsinnig? Was kann vielleicht?[13] — Von dieser schrecklichen Gewißheit bringst du mich mit keiner Hoffnung weg. — Ihr sollt mich hören, und ihr werdet: denn ich seh's, ihr seid bestürzt und könnt

---

[9] zu erringen, to wrestle for his possession.

[10] über die bekümmerten Gesichter ... fuhr wie ein Sonnenstrahl von seinem Angesichte ein Blick der Freude und Hoffnung, a look of joy and hope was reflected from his face, like a sunbeam, on your careworn features.

[11] sind müßig, are idle.

[12] Laßt sie nicht gewähren! Steuert dem Unheil! Do not let her have her own way! Stay the mischief.

[13] Was kann vielleicht? Possibly I might (go mad)?

euch selbst in euerm Busen nicht wiederfinden.[14] Laßt durch die gegenwärtige Gefahr nur einen Blick in das Vergangne dringen, das kurz Vergangne. Wendet eure Gedanken nach der Zukunft. Könnt ihr denn leben? Werdet ihr, wenn er zu Grunde geht? Mit seinem Athem flieht der letzte Hauch der Freiheit. Was war er euch? Für wen übergab er sich der dringendsten Gefahr? Seine Wunden flossen und heilten nur für euch. Die große Seele, die euch alle trug,[15] beschränkt ein Kerker, und Schauer tückischen Mordes schweben um sie her. Er denkt vielleicht an euch, er hofft auf euch, Er, der nur zu geben, nur zu erfüllen gewohnt war.

Zimmermeister. Gevatter, kommt.

Clärchen. Und ich habe nicht Arme, nicht Mark, wie ihr; doch hab' ich, was euch allen eben fehlt, Muth und Verachtung der Gefahr. Könnt' euch mein Athem doch entzünden! könnt' ich an meinen Busen drückend euch erwärmen und beleben! Kommt! In eurer Mitte will ich gehen! — Wie eine Fahne wehrlos ein edles Heer von Kriegern wehend anführt,[16] so soll mein Geist um eure Häupter flammen, und Liebe und Muth das schwankende, zerstreute Volk zu einem fürchterlichen Heer vereinigen.

Jetter. Schaff' sie bei Seite, sie dauert mich.

(Bürger ab.)

Brackenburg. Clärchen! siehst du nicht, wo wir sind?

Clärchen. Wo? Unter dem Himmel, der so oft sich herrlicher zu wölben schien,[17] wenn der Edle unter ihm herging. Aus diesen Fenstern haben sie herausgesehn, vier, fünf Köpfe über einander; an diesen Thüren haben sie gescharrt und genickt, wenn er auf die Memmen[18] herabsah. O, ich hatte sie so lieb,

---

[14] und könnt euch selbst in euerm Busen nicht wiederfinden, cannot recognise yourself in your heart.

[15] die euch alle trug, that bore you all.

[16] Wie eine Fahne wehrlos ein edles Heer von Kriegern wehend anführt, As the standard, fluttering, defenceless, leads a noble host of warriors.

[17] der so oft sich herrlicher zu wölben schien, that so often seemed a more glorious firmament.

[18] Memme, coward.

wie sie ihn ehrten! Wäre er Tyrann gewesen, möchten sie immer vor seinem Falle seitwärts gehn.[19] Aber sie liebten ihn! — O, ihr Hände, die ihr an die Mützen grifft, zum Schwert könnt ihr nicht greifen — Brackenburg, und wir? — Schelten wir sie? — Diese Arme, die ihn so oft fest hielten, was thun sie für ihn? List hat in der Welt so viel erreicht — Du kennst Wege und Stege,[20] kennst das alte Schloß. Es ist nichts unmöglich, gieb mir einen Anschlag.

Brackenburg. Wenn wir nach Hause gingen!

Clärchen. Gut.

Brackenburg. Dort an der Ecke seh' ich Alba's Wache; laß doch die St.mme der Vernunft dir zu Herzen dringen. Hältst du mich für feig? Glaubst du nicht, daß ich um deinetwillen sterben könnte? Hier sind wir beide toll, ich so gut wie du. Siehst du nicht das Unmögliche? Wenn du dich faßtest![21] Du bist außer dir.

Clärchen. Außer mir! Abscheulich! Brackenburg, ihr seid außer euch. Da ihr laut den Helden verehrtet, ihn Freund und Schutz und Hoffnung nanntet, ihm Vivat rieft, wenn er kam, da stand ich in meinem Winkel, schob das Fenster halb auf, verbarg mich lauschend, und das Herz schlug mir höher als euch allen. Jetzt schlägt mir's wieder höher als euch allen! Ihr verbergt euch, da es Noth ist, verläugnet ihn und fühlt nicht, daß ihr untergeht, wenn er verdirbt.

Brackenburg. Komm nach Hause.

Clärchen. Nach Hause?

Brackenburg. Besinne dich nur! Sieh dich um! Dies sind die Straßen, die du nur sonntäglich betratst, durch die du sittsam nach der Kirche gingst, wo du übertrieben ehrbar zürntest,[22] wenn ich mit einem freundlichen grüßenden Wort mich zu dir

[19] möchten sie immer vor seinem Falle seitwärts gehen, they might have stood aside at his fall.

[20] kennst Wege und Stege, know all the ways and by-paths.

[21] Wenn du dich faßtest! Oh, that you came to your senses.

[22] wo du übertrieben ehrbar zürntest, when you were angry with me from an excess of modesty.

gesellte. Du stehst und redest, handelst vor den Augen der offenen Welt; besinne dich, Liebe! wozu hilft es uns?

Clärchen. Nach Hause! Ja, ich besinne mich. Komm, Brackenburg, nach Hause! Weißt du, wo meine Heimath ist?

(Ab.)

Zweite Scene.

Gefängniß,

durch eine Lampe erhellt, ein Ruhebett im Grunde.

Egmont allein.

Alter Freund! immer getreuer Schlaf, fliehst du mich auch, wie die übrigen Freunde? Wie willig senktest du dich auf mein freies Haupt herunter und kühltest, wie ein schöner Myrtenkranz der Liebe, meine Schläfe! Mitten unter Waffen, auf der Woge des Lebens, ruht' ich leicht athmend, wie ein aufquellender Knabe,[1] in deinen Armen. Wenn Stürme durch Zweige und Blätter sausten, Ast und Wipfel sich knirrend bewegten, blieb innerst doch der Kern des Herzens ungeregt.[2] Was schüttelt dich nun? was erschüttert den festen treuen Sinn? Ich fühl's, es ist der Klang der Mordart, die an meiner Wurzel nascht.[3] Noch steh' ich aufrecht, und ein innrer Schauer durchfährt mich. Ja, sie überwindet, die verrätherische Gewalt; sie untergräbt den festen hohen Stamm, und eh' die Rinde dorrt, stürzt krachend und zerschmetternd deine Krone.

Warum denn jetzt, der du so oft gewalt'ge Sorgen gleich Seifenblasen dir vom Haupte weggewiesen,[4] warum vermagst du nicht die Ahnung zu verscheuchen, die tausendfach in dir sich auf

---

Second Scene.

[1] wie ein aufquellender Knabe, like a blooming boy.

[2] blieb innerst doch der Kern des Herzens ungeregt, the heart's core within me was unmoved.

[3] die an meiner Wurzel nascht, gnawing at my root.

[4] der du so oft gewalt'ge Sorgen gleich Seifenblasen dir vom Haupte weggewiesen, who so often hast blown tremendous cares like bubbles to the air.

und nieder treibt?[5] Seit wann begegnet der Tod dir fürchterlich? mit dessen wechselnden Bildern, wie mit den übrigen Gestalten der gewohnten Erde, du gelassen lebtest. — Auch ist Er's nicht, der rasche Feind, dem die gesunde Brust wetteifernd sich entgegen sehnt;[6] der Kerker ist's, des Grabes Vorbild,[7] dem Helden wie dem Feigen widerlich. Unleidlich ward mir's schon auf meinem gepolsterten Stuhle, wenn in stattlicher Versammlung die Fürsten, was leicht zu entscheiden war, mit wiederkehrenden Gesprächen überlegten, und zwischen düstern Wänden eines Saals die Balken der Decke mich erdrückten.[8] Da eilt' ich fort, sobald es möglich war, und rasch aufs Pferd mit tiefem Athemzuge. Und frisch hinaus, da wo wir hingehören! ins Feld, wo aus der Erde dampfend jede nächste Wohlthat der Natur, und durch die Himmel wehend alle Segen der Gestirne uns umwittern;[9] wo wir, dem erdgebornen Riesen gleich,[10] von der Berührung unsrer Mutter kräftiger uns in die Höhe reißen; wo wir die Menschheit ganz und menschliche Begier in allen Adern fühlen; wo das Verlangen vorzudringen, zu besiegen, zu erhaschen, seine Faust zu brauchen, zu besitzen, zu erobern, durch die Seele des jungen Jägers glüht; wo der Soldat sein angebornes Recht auf alle Welt mit raschem Schritt sich anmaßt,[11] und in fürchterlicher Freiheit wie ein Hagelwetter durch Wiese, Feld und Wald verderbend streicht,[12] und keine Grenzen kennt, die Menschenhand gezogen.

---

[5] die tausendfach in dir sich auf und nieder treibt, that in a thousand shapes recurs in your thoughts.

[6] wetteifernd sich entgegen sehnt, in its zeal yearns to meet.

[7] des Grabes Vorbild, the prototype of the grave.

[8] die Balken der Decke mich erdrückten, the roof-trees oppressed me.

[9] wo aus der Erde dampfend jede nächste Wohlthat der Natur, und durch die Himmel wehend alle Segen der Gestirne uns umwittern, where, steaming from the earth, every new blessing of nature, and, flashing through the heavens, all the blessings of the stars surround us.

[10] dem erdgebornen Riesen gleich, like the earth-born giant, i. e. Antæus.

[11] sein angebornes Recht auf alle Welt mit raschem Schritt sich anmaßt, with quick stride, claims his inborn (inherited) right of [commanding] all the world.

[12] wie ein Hagelwetter . . . verderbend streicht, like a hailstorm sweeps, destroying.

Du bist nur Bild, Erinnerungstraum des Glücks, das ich so lang' besessen; wo hat dich das Geschick verrätherisch hingeführt? Versagt es dir, den nie gescheuten Tod vorm Angesicht der Sonne rasch zu gönnen, um dir des Grabes Vorgeschmack in ekeln Moder zu bereiten?[13] Wie haucht er mich aus diesen Steinen widrig an! Schon starrt das Leben; vor dem Ruhebette, wie vor dem Grabe, scheut der Fuß. —

O Sorge! Sorge! die du vor der Zeit den Mord beginnst,[14] laß ab! — Seit wann ist Egmont denn allein, so ganz allein in dieser Welt? Dich macht der Zweifel fühllos, nicht das Glück. Ist die Gerechtigkeit des Königs, der du lebenslang vertrautest, ist der Regentin Freundschaft, die fast (du darfst es dir gestehn), fast Liebe war, sind sie auf einmal, wie ein glänzend Feuerbild der Nacht,[15] verschwunden? und lassen dich allein auf dunkelm Pfad zurück? Wird an der Spitze deiner Freunde Oranien nicht wagend sinnen?[16] Wird nicht ein Volk sich sammeln und mit anschwellender Gewalt den alten Freund erretten?

O, haltet, Mauern, die ihr mich einschließt, so vieler Geister wohlgemeintes Drängen nicht von mir ab; und welcher Muth aus meinen Augen sonst sich über sie ergoß, der kehre nun aus ihren Herzen in meines wieder.[17] O ja, sie rühren sich zu Tausenden! sie kommen! stehen mir zur Seite! Ihr frommer Wunsch eilt dringend zu dem Himmel, er bittet um ein Wunder. Und steigt zu meiner Rettung nicht ein Engel nieder, so seh' ich sie nach Lanz' und Schwertern greifen. Die Thore spalten sich,

---

[13] Versagt es dir, den nie gescheuten Tod vorm Angesicht der Sonne rasch zu gönnen, um dir des Grabes Vorgeschmack in ekeln Moder zu bereiten? Does it refuse to grant early in the light of day the never dreaded death, in order to prepare a foretaste of the grave in this horrible decaying prison?

[14] die du vor der Zeit den Mord beginnst, beginning your murderous work before the time.

[15] wie ein glänzend Feuerbild der Nacht, like a bright meteor of night.

[16] nicht wagend sinnen, not meditate a daring attempt.

[17] und welcher Muth aus meinen Augen sonst sich über sie ergoß, der kehre nun aus ihren Herzen in meines wieder, whatever courage they derived from (lit. was poured out over them by) my eyes, let it return now from their hearts into my own.

die Gitter springen, die Mauer stürzt vor ihren Händen ein, und der Freiheit des einbrechenden Tages steigt Egmont fröhlich entgegen. Wie manch bekannt Gesicht empfängt mich jauchzend! Ach Clärchen, wärst du Mann, so säh' ich dich gewiß auch hier zuerst und dankte dir, was einem Könige zu danken hart ist,[18] Freiheit.

Dritte Scene.

Clärchens Haus.

Clärchen

kommt mit einer Lampe und einem Glas Wasser aus der Kammer; sie setzt das Glas auf den Tisch und tritt ans Fenster.

Brackenburg? Seid ihr's? Was hört' ich denn? noch niemand? Es war niemand! Ich will die Lampe ins Fenster setzen, daß er sieht, ich wache noch, ich warte noch auf ihn. Er hat mir Nachricht versprochen. Nachricht? Entsetzliche Gewißheit! — Egmont verurtheilt! — Welch Gericht darf ihn fordern?[1] und sie verdammen ihn! Der König verdammt ihn? oder der Herzog? Und die Regentin entzieht sich! Oranien zaudert, und alle seine Freunde! — — Ist dies die Welt, von deren Wankelmuth, Unzuverlässigkeit[2] ich viel gehört und nichts empfunden habe? Ist dies die Welt? — Wer wäre bös' genug, den Theuern anzufeinden? Wäre Bosheit mächtig genug, den allgemein Erkannten schnell zu stürzen? Doch ist es so — es ist! — O Egmont, sicher hielt ich dich vor Gott und Menschen, wie in meinen Armen! Was war ich dir? Du hast mich dein genannt, mein ganzes Leben widmete ich deinem Leben — Was bin ich nun? Ver-

---

[18] was einem Könige zu danken hart ist, what it were hard to owe to a king.

Third Scene.

[1] darf ihn fordern, dare claim him (as knight of the Golden Fleece).

[2] Wankelmuth, Unzuverlässigkeit, changeable disposition, not to be depended upon.

gebens streck' ich nach der Schlinge, die dich faßt, die Hand aus. Du hülflos, und ich frei! — Hier ist der Schlüssel zu meiner Thüre. An meiner Willkür hängt mein Gehen und mein Kommen, und dir bin ich zu nichts![3] — — O, bindet mich, damit ich nicht verzweifle; und werft mich in den tiefsten Kerker, daß ich das Haupt an feuchte Mauern schlage, nach Freiheit winsle,[4] träume, wie ich ihm helfen wollte, wenn Fesseln mich nicht lähmten, wie ich ihm helfen würde. — Nun bin ich frei! Und in der Freiheit liegt die Angst der Ohnmacht.[5] — Mir selbst bewußt, nicht fähig, ein Glied nach seiner Hülfe zu rühren. Ach leider, auch der kleine Theil von deinem Wesen, dein Clärchen, ist wie du gefangen und regt getrennt im Todeskrampfe nur die letzten Kräfte. — Ich höre schleichen, husten — Brackenburg — Er ist's! — Elender guter Mann, dein Schicksal bleibt sich immer gleich; dein Liebchen öffnet dir die nächtliche Thür, und ach! zu welch unseliger Zusammenkunft![6]

Brackenburg tritt auf.

Clärchen. Du kommst so bleich und schüchtern, Brackenburg! was ist's?

Brackenburg. Durch Umwege und Gefahren such' ich dich auf. Die großen Straßen sind besetzt; durch Gäßchen und durch Winkel hab' ich mich zu dir gestohlen.

Clärchen. Erzähl', wie ist's?

Brackenburg (indem er sich setzt). Ach, Cläre, laß mich weinen. Ich liebt' ihn nicht. Er war der reiche Mann und lockte des Armen einziges Schaf zur bessern Weide herüber.[7] Ich hab' ihn nie verflucht; Gott hat mich treu geschaffen und weich. In Schmerzen floß mein Leben von mir nieder, und zu verschmachten hofft' ich jeden Tag.

---

[3] dir bin ich zu nichts, I am nothing (of no avail) to you.

[4] nach Freiheit winsle, sigh for liberty.

[5] liegt die Angst der Ohnmacht, lies the anguish of impotence.

[6] zu welch unseliger Zusammenkunft, to what a wretched meeting.

[7] und lockte des Armen einziges Schaf zur bessern Weide herüber, enticed to better pastures the sheep of the poor man (2 Samuel xii. 3, 4).

Clärchen. Vergiß das, Brackenburg! Vergiß dich selbst. Sprich mir von ihm! Ist's wahr? Ist er verurtheilt?

Brackenburg. Er ist's! ich weiß es ganz genau.

Clärchen. Und lebt noch?

Brackenburg. Ja, er lebt noch.

Clärchen. Wie willst du das versichern? — Die Tyrannei ermordet in der Nacht den Herrlichen! vor allen Augen verborgen fließt sein Blut. Aengstlich im Schlafe liegt das betäubte Volk und träumt von Rettung, träumt ihres ohnmächtigen Wunsches Erfüllung, indeß, unwillig über uns, sein Geist die Welt verläßt. Er ist dahin! — Täusche mich nicht! dich nicht!

Brackenburg. Nein, gewiß, er lebt! — Und leider! es bereitet der Spanier dem Volke, das er zertreten[8] will, ein fürchterliches Schauspiel, gewaltsam jedes Herz, das nach Freiheit sich regt, auf ewig zu zerknirschen.[9]

Clärchen. Fahre fort und sprich gelassen auch mein Todesurtheil aus! Ich wandle den seligen Gefilden schon näher und näher, mir weht der Trost aus jenen Gegenden des Friedens[10] schon herüber. Sag' an.

Brackenburg. Ich konnt' es an den Wachen merken, aus Reden, die bald da bald dort fielen, daß auf dem Markte geheimnißvoll ein Schreckniß zubereitet werde. Ich schlich durch Seitenwege, durch bekannte Gänge nach meines Vettern Hause und sah aus einem Hinterfenster nach dem Markte. — Es wehten Fackeln in einem weiten Kreise spanischer Soldaten hin und wieder. Ich schärfte mein ungewohntes Auge, und aus der Nacht stieg mir ein schwarzes Gerüst entgegen, geräumig, hoch; mir grauste vor dem Anblick. Geschäftig waren viele rings umher bemüht, was noch von Holzwerk weiß und sichtbar war, mit schwarzem Tuch einhüllend zu verkleiden.[11] Die Treppen deckten sie zuletzt auch schwarz, ich sah es wohl. Sie schienen

---

[8] zertreten, stamp down.

[9] auf ewig zu zerknirschen, to crush for ever.

[10] aus jenen Gegenden des Friedens, from yonder regions of peace; the Elysian fields.

[11] einhüllend zu verkleiden, hide by wrapping in.

die Weihe eines gräßlichen Opfers vorbereitend zu begehn.[12] Ein weißes Crucifix, das durch die Nacht wie Silber blinkte, ward an der einen Seite hoch aufgesteckt. Ich sah, und sah die schreckliche Gewißheit immer gewisser. Noch wankten Fackeln hie und da herum; allmählig wichen sie und erloschen. Auf einmal war die scheußliche Geburt der Nacht in ihrer Mutter Schooß zurückgekehrt.[13]

Clärchen. Still, Brackenburg! Nun still! Laß diese Hülle auf meiner Seele ruhn. Verschwunden sind die Gespenster,[14] und du, holde Nacht, leih' deinen Mantel der Erde, die in sich gährt;[15] sie trägt nicht länger die abscheuliche Last, reißt ihre tiefen Spalten grausend auf und knirscht das Mordgerüst hinunter.[16] Und irgend einen Engel sendet der Gott, den sie zum Zeugen ihrer Wuth geschändet;[17] vor des Boten heiliger Berührung lösen sich Riegel und Bande, und er umgießt den Freund mit mildem Schimmer; er führt ihn durch die Nacht zur Freiheit sanft und still. Und auch mein Weg geht heimlich in dieser Dunkelheit, ihm zu begegnen.

Brackenburg (sie aufhaltend). Mein Kind, wohin? was wagst du?

Clärchen. Leise, Lieber, daß niemand erwache! daß wir uns selbst nicht wecken! Kennst du dies Fläschchen, Brackenburg? Ich nahm dir's scherzend, als du mit übereiltem Tod' oft ungeduldig drohtest. — Und nun, mein Freund —

Brackenburg. In aller Heiligen Namen! —

Clärchen. Du hinderst nichts. Tod ist mein Theil! und gönne mir den sanften schnellen Tod, den du dir selbst bereitetest. Gieb mir deine Hand! — Im Augenblick, da ich die dunkle

---

[12] Sie schienen die Weihe —— begehn, they appeared to prepare the celebration of the consecration of a horrible immolation.

[13] Auf einmal war die scheußliche Geburt —— zurückgekehrt, at once the horrible birth (creation, creature) of night had returned into her mother's womb.

[14] Gespenster, ghosts.

[15] in sich gährt, ferments within.

[16] knirscht das Mordgerüst hinunter, swallows crashing the murderous pile.

[17] den sie zum Zeugen ihrer Wuth geschändet, whom they have dishonoured [by making him] the witness of their rage.

Pforte eröffne, aus der kein Rückweg ist, könnt' ich mit diesem Händedruck dir sagen: wie sehr ich dich geliebt, wie sehr ich dich bejammert. Mein Bruder starb mir jung; dich wählt' ich, seine Stelle zu ersetzen. Es widersprach dein Herz und quälte sich und mich,[18] verlangtest heiß und immer heißer, was dir nicht beschieden war. Vergieb mir und leb' wohl! Laß mich dich Bruder nennen! Es ist ein Name, der viel Namen in sich faßt. Nimm die letzte schöne Blume der Scheidenden mit treuem Herzen ab[19] — nimm diesen Kuß — Der Tod vereinigt alles, Brackenburg, uns denn auch.

Brackenburg. So laß mich mit dir sterben! Theile! Theile! Es ist genug, zwei Leben auszulöschen.

Clärchen. Bleib! du sollst leben, du kannst leben. — Steh meiner Mutter bei, die ohne dich in Armuth sich verzehren würde.[20] Sei ihr, was ich ihr nicht mehr sein kann; lebt zusammen und beweint mich. Beweint das Vaterland und den, der es allein erhalten konnte. Das heutige Geschlecht wird diesen Jammer nicht los;[21] die Wuth der Rache selbst vermag ihn nicht zu tilgen. Lebt, ihr Armen, die Zeit noch hin, die keine Zeit mehr ist. Heut steht die Welt auf einmal still; es stockt ihr Kreislauf,[22] und mein Puls schlägt kaum noch wenige Minuten. Leb' wohl!

Brackenburg. O, lebe du mit uns, wie wir für dich allein! Du tödtest uns in dir, o, leb' und leide. Wir wollen unzertrennlich dir zu beiden Seiten stehn, und immer achtsam soll die Liebe den schönsten Trost in ihren lebendigen Armen dir bereiten. Sei unser! Unser! Ich darf nicht sagen, mein.

Clärchen. Leise, Brackenburg! Du fühlst nicht, was du rührst. Wo Hoffnung dir erscheint, ist mir Verzweiflung.

---

18 quälte sich und mich, tormented itself and me.

19 Nimm die letzte schöne Blume der Scheidenden mit treuem Herzen ab, Gather the last fair flower of the parting one with faithful heart.

20 sich verzehren würde, would perish.

21 das heutige Geschlecht wird diesen Jammer nicht los, the present generation will not be rid of this woe.

22 es stockt ihr Kreislauf, stands still in her orbit.

Brackenburg. Theile mit den Lebendigen die Hoffnung! Verweil' am Rande des Abgrunds, schau' hinab und sieh auf uns zurück.

Clärchen. Ich hab' überwunden,[23] ruf' mich nicht wieder zum Streit.

Brackenburg. Du bist betäubt; gehüllt in Nacht, suchst du die Tiefe. Noch ist nicht jedes Licht erloschen, noch mancher Tag! —

Clärchen. Weh! über dich Weh! Weh! Grausam zerreißest du den Vorhang vor meinem Auge. Ja, er wird grauen, der Tag! vergebens alle Nebel um sich ziehn[24] und wider Willen grauen! Furchtsam schaut der Bürger aus seinem Fenster, die Nacht läßt einen schwarzen Flecken zurück; er schaut, und fürchterlich wächst im Lichte das Mordgerüst. Neuleidend wendet das entweihte Gottesbild sein flehend Auge zum Vater auf.[25] Die Sonne wagt sich nicht hervor; sie will die Stunde nicht bezeichnen, in der er sterben soll. Träge gehn die Zeiger ihren Weg, und eine Stunde nach der andern schlägt. Halt! Halt! Nun ist es Zeit! mich scheucht des Morgens Ahnung in das Grab.[26] (Sie tritt ans Fenster, als sähe sie sich um, und trinkt heimlich.)

Brackenburg. Cläre! Cläre!

Clärchen (geht nach dem Tisch und trinkt das Wasser). Hier ist der Rest! Ich locke dich nicht nach. Thu', was du darfst, leb' wohl. Lösche diese Lampe still und ohne Zaudern, ich geh' zur Ruhe. Schleiche dich sachte weg, ziehe die Thür nach dir zu. Still! Wecke meine Mutter nicht! Geh, rette dich! Rette dich, wenn du nicht mein Mörder scheinen willst.

(Ab.)

Brackenburg. Sie läßt mich zum letztenmale, wie immer.

---

[23] überwunden, conquered.

[24] vergebens alle Nebel um sich ziehn, in vain draw round him all the mists.

[25] Neuleidend wendet das entweihte Gottesbild sein flehend Auge zum Vater auf, Newly, again suffering, the desecrated image of God turns an entreating eye upon the Father.

[26] mich scheucht des Morgens Ahnung in das Grab, the suspicion of the morning [being at hand] drives me into the grave.

O, könnte eine Menschenseele fühlen, wie sie ein liebend Herz zerreißen kann. Sie läßt mich stehn, mir selber überlassen; und Tod und Leben ist mir gleich verhaßt. — Allein zu sterben! — Weint, ihr Liebenden! Kein härter Schicksal ist als meins! Sie theilt mit mir den Todestropfen, und schickt mich weg! von ihrer Seite weg! Sie zieht mich nach, und stößt ins Leben mich zurück. O Egmont, welch preiswürdig Loos fällt dir![27] Sie geht voran; der Kranz des Siegs aus ihrer Hand ist dein, sie bringt den ganzen Himmel dir entgegen! — Und soll ich folgen? wieder seitwärts stehn? den unauslöschlichen Neid[28] in jene Wohnungen hinübertragen? — Auf Erden ist kein Bleiben mehr für mich, und Höll' und Himmel bieten gleiche Qual. Wie wäre der Vernichtung Schreckenshand dem Unglückseligen willkommen![29]

Brackenburg geht ab; das Theater bleibt einige Zeit unverändert. Eine Musik, Clärchens Tod bezeichnend, beginnt; die Lampe, welche Brackenburg auszulöschen vergessen, flammt noch einigemal auf, dann erlischt sie. Bald verwandelt sich der Schauplatz in das Gefängniß.

Vierte Scene.

Gefängniß.

Egmont liegt schlafend auf dem Ruhebette. Es entsteht ein Gerassel mit Schlüsseln, und die Thür thut sich auf. Diener mit Fackeln treten herein; ihnen folgt Ferdinand, Alba's Sohn, und Silva, begleitet von Gewaffneten. Egmont fährt aus dem Schlaf auf.

Egmont. Wer seid ihr, die ihr mir unfreundlich den Schlaf von den Augen schüttelt? Was künden eure trotzigen, unsichern

---

[27] welch preiswürdig Loos fällt dir! what enviable, lit. praiseworthy, fate is thine.

[28] unauslöschlichen Neid, inextinguishable envy.

[29] Wie wäre der Vernichtung Schreckenshand dem Unglückseligen willkommen! How welcome would be the terrible hand of annihilation to the wretched.

Blicke mir an? Warum diesen fürchterlichen Aufzug?[1] Welchen Schreckenstraum kommt ihr der halberwachten Seele vorzulügen?

Silva. Uns schickt der Herzog, dir dein Urtheil anzukündigen.

Egmont. Bringst du den Henker auch mit, es zu vollziehen?

Silva. Vernimm es, so wirst du wissen, was deiner wartet.

Egmont. So ziemt es euch und euerm schändlichen Beginnen! In Nacht gebrütet[2] und in Nacht vollführt. So mag diese freche That der Ungerechtigkeit sich verbergen! — Tritt kühn hervor, der du das Schwert verhüllt unter dem Mantel trägst; hier ist mein Haupt, das freieste, das je die Tyrannei vom Rumpf gerissen.

Silva. Du irrst! Was gerechte Richter beschließen, werden sie vorm Angesicht des Tages nicht verbergen.

Egmont. So übersteigt die Frechheit jeden Begriff und Gedanken.

Silva (nimmt einem Dabeistehenden das Urtheil ab, entfaltet's und liest). „Im Namen des Königs, und kraft besonderer von seiner Majestät uns übertragenen Gewalt,[3] alle seine Unterthanen, weß Standes sie seien, zugleich die Ritter des goldnen Vließes zu richten, erkennen wir —"

Egmont. Kann die der König übertragen?

Silva. „Erkennen wir, nach vorgängiger genauer, gesetzlicher Untersuchung, Dich Heinrich Grafen Egmont, Prinzen von Gaure, des Hochverrathes schuldig, und sprechen das Urtheil: daß du mit der Frühe des einbrechenden Morgens aus dem Kerker auf den Markt geführt, und dort vorm Angesicht des Volks zur Warnung aller Verräther mit dem Schwerte vom Leben zum Tod gebracht

---

Fourth Scene.

[1] fürchterlichen Aufzug, dreadful display.

[2] gebrütet, hatched.

[3] kraft besonderer von seiner Majestät uns übertragenen Gewalt, in virtue of special power delegated to us by his majesty.

werden sollest. Gegeben Brüssel am“ (Datum und Jahrzahl werden undeutlich gelesen, so, daß sie der Zuhörer nicht versteht.)

„Ferdinand, Herzog von Alba, Vorsitzer des Gerichts der Zwölfe.“

Du weißt nun dein Schicksal; es bleibt dir wenige Zeit, dich drein zu ergeben,[4] dein Haus zu bestellen und von den Deinigen Abschied zu nehmen.

(Silva mit dem Gefolge geht ab. Es bleibt Ferdinand und zwei Fackeln; das Theater ist mäßig erleuchtet.)

Egmont (hat eine Weile, in sich versenkt, stille gestanden und Silva, ohne sich umzusehen, abgehn lassen. Er glaubt sich allein, und da er die Augen aufhebt, erblickt er Alba's Sohn). Du stehst und bleibst? Willst du mein Erstaunen, mein Entsetzen noch durch deine Gegenwart vermehren? Willst du noch etwa die willkommene Botschaft deinem Vater bringen, daß ich unmännlich verzweifle? Geh! Sag' ihm! Sag' ihm, daß er weder mich noch die Welt belügt. Ihm, dem Ruhmsüchtigen, wird man es erst hinter den Schultern leise lispeln, dann laut und lauter sagen, und wenn er einst von diesem Gipfel herabsteigt,[5] werden tausend Stimmen es ihm entgegen rufen: Nicht das Wohl des Staats, nicht die Würde des Königs, nicht die Ruhe der Provinzen haben ihn hierher gebracht. Um sein selbst willen hat er Krieg gerathen, daß der Krieger im Kriege gelte. Er hat diese ungeheure Verwirrung erregt,[6] damit man seiner bedürfe. Und ich falle, ein Opfer seines niedrigen Hasses, seines kleinlichen Neides. Ja, ich weiß es, und ich darf es sagen: der Sterbende, der tödtlich Verwundete kann es sagen: mich hat der Eingebildete beneidet; mich wegzutilgen[7] hat er lange gesonnen und gedacht.

Schon damals, als wir noch jünger mit Würfeln spielten,

---

[4] dich drein zu ergeben, to reconcile yourself to your fate.

[5] wenn er einst von diesem Gipfel herabsteigt. A prophetical reference to the disgrace in which Alva was for a time involved after his return to Spain.

[6] er hat diese ungeheure Verwirrung erregt, he has caused this tremendous confusion.

[7] wegzutilgen, to destroy.

und die Haufen Goldes, einer nach dem andern, von seiner Seite zu mir herübereilten, da stand er grimmig, log Gelassenheit, und innerlich verzehrt' ihn die Aergerniß,[8] mehr über mein Glück, als über seinen Verlust. Noch erinnere ich mich des funkelnden Blicks, der verrätherischen Blässe, als wir an einem öffentlichen Feste vor vielen tausend Menschen um die Wette schossen. Er forderte mich auf,[9] und beide Nationen standen; die Spanier, die Niederländer wetteten und wünschten. Ich überwand ihn; seine Kugel irrte, die meine traf; ein lauter Freudenschrei der Meinigen durchbrach die Luft. Nun trifft mich sein Geschoß. Sag' ihm, daß ich's weiß, daß ich ihn kenne, daß die Welt jede Siegszeichen verachtet, die ein kleiner Geist erschleichend sich aufrichtet.[10] Und du! wenn einem Sohne möglich ist, von der Sitte des Vaters zu weichen, übe bei Zeiten die Scham, indem du dich für den schämst, den du gerne von ganzem Herzen verehren möchtest.

Ferdinand. Ich höre dich an, ohne dich zu unterbrechen! Deine Vorwürfe lasten wie Keulschläge auf einen Helm; ich fühle die Erschütterung, aber ich bin bewaffnet. Du triffst mich, du verwundest mich nicht; fühlbar ist mir allein der Schmerz, der mir den Busen zerreißt. Wehe mir! Wehe! Zu einem solchen Anblick bin ich aufgewachsen, zu einem solchen Schauspiele bin ich gesendet!

Egmont. Du brichst in Klagen aus? Was rührt, was bekümmert dich? Ist es eine späte Reue, daß du der schändlichen Verschwörung deinen Dienst geliehen? Du bist so jung und hast ein glückliches Ansehn. Du warst so zutraulich, so freundlich gegen mich. So lang' ich dich sah, war ich mit deinem Vater versöhnt. Und eben so verstellt,[11] verstellter als er, lockst du mich in das Netz. Du bist der Abscheuliche! Wer Ihm traut,

---

[8] innerlich verzehrt' ihn die Aergerniß, his heart was consumed by vexation.

[9] Er forderte mich auf, he challenged me.

[10] die ein kleiner Geist erschleichend sich aufrichtet, which a small mind stealthily erects to his glory.

[11] Und eben so verstellt, and as cunningly.

mag er es auf seine Gefahr thun; aber wer fürchtete Gefahr, dir zu vertrauen? Geh! Geh! Raube mir nicht die wenigen Augenblicke! Geh, daß ich mich sammle, die Welt und dich zuerst vergesse! —

Ferdinand. Was soll ich dir sagen? Ich stehe und sehe dich an, und sehe dich nicht, und fühle mich nicht. Soll ich mich entschuldigen? Soll ich dir versichern, daß ich erst spät, erst ganz zuletzt des Vaters Absichten erfuhr, daß ich als ein gezwungenes, ein lebloses Werkzeug[12] seines Willens handelte? Was fruchtet's, welche Meinung du von mir haben magst? Du bist verloren; und ich Unglücklicher stehe nur da, um dir's zu versichern, um dich zu bejammern.

Egmont. Welche sonderbare Stimme, welch ein unerwarteter Trost begegnet mir auf dem Wege zum Grabe? Du, Sohn meines ersten, meines fast einzigen Feindes, du bedauerst mich, du bist nicht unter meinen Mördern? Sage, rede! Für wen soll ich dich halten?

Ferdinand. Grausamer Vater! Ja, ich erkenne dich in diesem Befehle. Du kanntest mein Herz, meine Gesinnung, die du so oft als Erbtheil einer zärtlichen Mutter schaltest. Mich dir gleich zu bilden, sandtest du mich hierher. Diesen Mann am Rande des gähnenden Grabes, in der Gewalt eines willkürlichen Todes zu sehen zwingst du mich, daß ich den tiefsten Schmerz empfinde, daß ich taub gegen alles Schicksal, daß ich unempfindlich werde, es geschehe mir was wolle.[13]

Egmont. Ich erstaune! Fasse dich! Stehe, rede wie ein Mann.

Ferdinand. O daß ich ein Weib wäre! daß man mir sagen könnte: was rührt dich? was ficht dich an?[14] Sage mir ein größeres, ein ungeheureres Uebel, mache mich zum Zeugen einer schrecklichern That; ich will dir danken, ich will sagen: es war nichts.

---

[12] lebloses Werkzeug, lifeless instrument.

[13] es geschehe mir was wolle, happen to me what may.

[14] was ficht dich an? what troubles you?

Egmont. Du verlierst dich. Wo bist du?

Ferdinand. Laß diese Leidenschaft rasen, laß mich losgebunden klagen! Ich will nicht standhaft scheinen, wenn alles in mir zusammenbricht. Dich soll ich hier sehn? — Dich? — es ist entsetzlich! Du verstehst mich nicht! Und sollst du mich verstehen? Egmont! Egmont! (Ihm um den Hals fallend.)

Egmont. Löse mir das Geheimniß.[15]

Ferdinand. Kein Geheimniß.

Egmont. Wie bewegt dich so tief das Schicksal eines fremden Mannes?

Ferdinand. Nicht fremd! Du bist mir nicht fremd. Dein Name war's, der mir in meiner ersten Jugend gleich einem Stern des Himmels entgegenleuchtete. Wie oft hab' ich nach dir gehorcht, gefragt! Des Kindes Hoffnung ist der Jüngling, des Jünglings der Mann. So bist du vor mir her geschritten; immer vor, und ohne Neid sah ich dich vor, und schritt dir nach, und fort und fort. Nun hofft' ich endlich dich zu sehen, und sah dich, und mein Herz flog dir entgegen.[16] Dich hatt' ich mir bestimmt, und wählte dich aufs neue, da ich dich sah. Nun hofft' ich erst mit dir zu sein, mit dir zu leben, dich zu fassen, dich — Das ist nun alles weggeschnitten, und ich sehe dich hier!

Egmont. Mein Freund, wenn es dir wohl thun kann, so nimm die Versicherung, daß im ersten Augenblick mein Gemüth dir entgegenkam. Und höre mich. Laß uns ein ruhiges Wort unter einander wechseln. Sage mir: ist es der strenge, ernste Wille deines Vaters, mich zu tödten?

Ferdinand. Er ist's.

Egmont. Dieses Urtheil wäre nicht ein leeres Schreckbild, mich zu ängstigen, durch Furcht und Drohung zu strafen, mich zu erniedrigen, und dann mit königlicher Gnade mich wieder aufzuheben?

Ferdinand. Nein, ach leider nein! Anfangs schmeichelte

---

[15] Löse mir das Geheimniß, Solve the riddle.

[16] mein Herz flog dir entgegen, my heart yearned towards thee.

ich mir selbst mit dieser ausweichenden Hoffnung;[17] und schon da empfand ich Angst und Schmerz, dich in diesem Zustande zu sehen. Nun ist es wirklich, ist gewiß. Nein, ich regiere mich nicht. Wer giebt mir eine Hülfe, wer einen Rath, dem Unvermeidlichen zu entgehen?

Egmont. So höre mich. Wenn deine Seele so gewaltsam dringt, mich zu retten, wenn du die Uebermacht verabscheust, die mich gefesselt hält, so rette mich! Die Augenblicke sind kostbar. Du bist des Allgewaltigen Sohn, und selbst gewaltig — Laß uns entfliehen! Ich kenne die Wege; die Mittel können dir nicht unbekannt sein. Nur diese Mauern, nur wenige Meilen entfernen mich von meinen Freunden. Löse diese Bande, bringe mich zu ihnen und sei unser. Gewiß, der König dankt dir dereinst meine Rettung. Jetzt ist er überrascht, und vielleicht ist ihm alles unbekannt. Dein Vater wagt; und die Majestät muß das Geschehene billigen, wenn sie sich auch davor entsetzet. Du denkst? O, denke mir den Weg der Freiheit aus! Sprich und nähre die Hoffnung der lebendigen Seele.

Ferdinand. Schweig'! o, schweige! Du vermehrst mit jedem Worte meine Verzweiflung. Hier ist kein Ausweg, kein Rath, keine Flucht. — Das quält mich, das greift und faßt mir wie mit Klauen die Brust. Ich habe selbst das Netz zusammengezogen; ich kenne die strengen festen Knoten; ich weiß, wie jeder Kühnheit, jeder List die Wege verrennt sind;[18] ich fühle mich mit dir und mit allen andern gefesselt. Würde ich klagen, hätte ich nicht alles versucht? Zu seinen Füßen habe ich gelegen, geredet und gebeten. Er schickte mich hierher, um alles, was von Lebenslust und Freude mit mir lebt, in diesem Augenblicke zu zerstören.

Egmont. Und keine Rettung?

Ferdinand. Keine!

Egmont (mit dem Fuße stampfend). Keine Rettung! —

---

[17] ausweichenden Hoffnung, delusive hope.

[18] die Wege verrennt sind, ways are barred.

— Süßes Leben! Schöne freundliche Gewohnheit des Daseins und Wirkens![19] von dir soll ich scheiden! So gelassen scheiden! Nicht im Tumulte der Schlacht, unter dem Geräusch der Waffen, in der Zerstreuung des Getümmels giebst du mir ein flüchtiges Lebewohl; du nimmst keinen eiligen Abschied, verkürzest nicht den Augenblick der Trennung. Ich soll deine Hand fassen, dir noch einmal in die Augen sehn, deine Schöne,[20] deinen Werth recht lebhaft fühlen, und dann mich entschlossen losreißen und sagen: Fahre hin!

Ferdinand. Und ich soll daneben stehn, zusehn, dich nicht halten, nicht hindern können! O welche Stimme reichte zur Klage! Welches Herz flösse nicht aus seinen Banden[21] vor diesem Jammer?

Egmont. Fasse dich!

Ferdinand. Du kannst dich fassen, du kannst entsagen, den schweren Schritt an der Hand der Nothwendigkeit heldenmäßig gehn. Was kann ich? Was soll ich? Du überwindest dich selbst und uns; du überstehst;[22] ich überlebe dich und mich selbst. Bei der Freude des Mahls hab' ich mein Licht, im Getümmel der Schlacht meine Fahne verloren. Schal, verworren, trüb'[23] scheint mir die Zukunft.

Egmont. Junger Freund, den ich durch ein sonderbares Schicksal zugleich gewinne und verliere, der für mich die Todesschmerzen empfindet, für mich leidet, sieh mich in diesen Augenblicken an; du verlierst mich nicht. War dir mein Leben ein Spiegel, in welchem du dich gerne betrachtetest, so sei es auch mein Tod. Die Menschen sind nicht nur zusammen, wenn sie beisammen sind;[24] auch der Entfernte, der Abgeschiedne lebt uns.

---

19 Schöne freundliche Gewohnheit des Daseins und Wirkens! Fair pleasant habit of being and working.

20 Schöne, i. q. Schönheit.

21 flösse nicht aus seinen Banden, would not melt.

22 du überstehst, you are past suffering.

23 Schal, verworren, trüb', insipid, confused, and dim.

24 sind nicht nur zusammen, wenn sie beisammen sind, are not only together when actually living together.

Ich lebe dir und habe mir genug gelebt. Eines jeden Tages hab' ich mich gefreut; an jedem Tage mit rascher Wirkung meine Pflicht gethan, wie mein Gewissen mir sie zeigte. Nun endigt sich das Leben, wie es sich früher, früher, schon auf dem Sande von Gravelingen hätte endigen können. Ich höre auf zu leben; aber ich habe gelebt. So leb' auch du, mein Freund, gern und mit Lust und scheue den Tod nicht.

Ferdinand. Du hättest dich für uns erhalten können, erhalten sollen. Du hast dich selber getödtet. Oft hört' ich, wenn kluge Männer über dich sprachen, feindselige, wohlwollende, sie stritten lang' über deinen Werth; doch endlich vereinigten sie sich, keiner wagt' es zu läugnen, jeder gestand: ja, er wandelt einen gefährlichen Weg. Wie oft wünscht' ich, dich warnen zu können! Hattest du denn keine Freunde?

Egmont. Ich war gewarnt.

Ferdinand. Und wie ich punktweise alle diese Beschuldigungen wieder in der Anklage fand, und deine Antworten! Gut genug, dich zu entschuldigen; nicht triftig genug,[25] dich von der Schuld zu befreien —

Egmont. Dies sei bei Seite gelegt. Es glaubt der Mensch sein Leben zu leiten, sich selbst zu führen; und sein Innerstes wird unwiderstehlich nach seinem Schicksale gezogen.[26] Laß uns darüber nicht sinnen; dieser Gedanken entschlag' ich mich leicht — schwerer der Sorge für dieses Land; doch auch dafür wird gesorgt sein. Kann mein Blut für viele fließen, meinem Volke Friede bringen, so fließt es willig. Leider wird's nicht so werden. Doch es ziemt dem Menschen, nicht mehr zu grübeln, wo er nicht mehr wirken soll. Kannst du die verderbende Gewalt deines Vaters aufhalten, lenken, so thu's. Wer wird das können? — Leb' wohl!

Ferdinand. Ich kann nicht gehn.

---

[25] nicht triftig genug, not valid enough.

[26] unwiderstehlich nach seinem Schicksale gezogen, irresistibly drawn by fate.

Egmont. Laß meine Leute dir aufs beste empfohlen sein! Ich habe gute Menschen zu Dienern; daß sie nicht zerstreut, nicht unglücklich werden! Wie steht es um Richard, meinen Schreiber?

Ferdinand. Er ist dir vorangegangen. Sie haben ihn als Mitschuldigen des Hochverraths enthauptet.

Egmont. Arme Seele! — Noch Eins, und dann leb' wohl, ich kann nicht mehr. Was auch den Geist gewaltsam beschäftigt, fordert die Natur zuletzt doch unwiderstehlich ihre Rechte, und wie ein Kind, umwunden von der Schlange,[27] des erquickenden Schlafs genießt, so legt der Müde sich noch einmal vor der Pforte des Todes nieder und ruht tief aus, als ob er einen weiten Weg zu wandern hätte. — Noch Eins — Ich kenne ein Mädchen, du wirst sie nicht verachten, weil sie mein war. Nun ich sie dir empfehle, sterb' ich ruhig. Du bist ein edler Mann; ein Weib, das den findet, ist geborgen. Lebt mein alter Adolph? ist er frei?

Ferdinand. Der muntere Greis, der euch zu Pferde immer begleitete?

Egmont. Derselbe.

Ferdinand. Er lebt, er ist frei.

Egmont. Er weiß ihre Wohnung; laß dich von ihm führen, und lohn' ihm bis an sein Ende, daß er dir den Weg zu diesem Kleinode zeigt. — Leb' wohl!

Ferdinand. Ich gehe nicht.

Egmont (ihn nach der Thür drängend). Leb' wohl!

Ferdinand. O, laß mich noch!

Egmont. Freund, keinen Abschied.

(Er begleitet Ferdinanden bis an die Thür und reißt sich dort von ihm los. Ferdinand, betäubt, entfernt sich eilend.)

Egmont (allein). Feindseliger Mann! Du glaubtest nicht, mir diese Wohlthat durch deinen Sohn zu erzeigen. Durch ihn bin ich der Sorgen los und der Schmerzen, der Furcht und jedes

---

[27] umwunden von der Schlange, in the folds of the snake.

ängstlichen Gefühls. Sanft und dringend fordert die Natur ihren letzten Zoll. Es ist vorbei, es ist beschlossen! und was die letzte Nacht mich ungewiß auf meinem Lager wachend hielt, das schläfert nun mit unbezwinglicher Gewißheit meine Sinnen ein.[28]

(Er setzt sich aufs Ruhebett. Musik.)

Süßer Schlaf! Du kommst, wie ein reines Glück, ungebeten, unerfleht am willigsten. Du lösest die Knoten der strengen Gedanken, vermischest alle Bilder der Freude und des Schmerzes; ungehindert fließt der Kreis innerer Harmonien, und eingehüllt in gefälligen Wahnsinn,[29] versinken wir und hören auf zu sein.

(Er entschläft; die Musik begleitet seinen Schlummer. Hinter seinem Lager scheint sich die Mauer zu eröffnen, eine glänzende Erscheinung zeigt sich. Die Freiheit in himmlischem Gewande, von einer Klarheit umflossen, ruht auf einer Wolke. Sie hat die Züge von Clärchen und neigt sich gegen den schlafenden Helden. Sie drückt eine bedauernde Empfindung aus, sie scheint ihn zu beklagen. Bald faßt sie sich, und mit aufmunternder Geberde zeigt sie ihm das Bündel Pfeile,[30] dann den Stab mit dem Hute. Sie heißt ihn froh sein, und indem sie ihm andeutet, daß sein Tod den Provinzen die Freiheit verschaffen werde, erkennt sie ihn als Sieger und reicht ihm einen Lorbeerkranz. Wie sie sich mit dem Kranze dem Haupte nahet, macht Egmont eine Bewegung, wie einer, der sich im Schlafe regt, dergestalt, daß er mit dem Gesicht aufwärts gegen sie liegt. Sie hält den Kranz über seinem Haupte schwebend: man hört ganz von weitem eine kriegerische Musik von Trommeln und Pfeifen: bei dem leisesten Laut derselben verschwindet die Erscheinung. Der Schall wird stärker. Egmont erwacht; das Gefängniß wird vom Morgen mäßig erhellt. Seine erste Bewegung ist, nach dem Haupte zu greifen: er steht auf und sieht sich um, indem er die Hand auf dem Haupte behält.)

Verschwunden ist der Kranz! Du schönes Bild, das Licht des Tages hat dich verscheucht! Ja, sie waren's, sie waren vereint, die

---

[28] schläfert mit unbezwinglicher Gewißheit meine Sinnen ein, wraps irresistibly my senses in slumber.

[29] eingehüllt in gefälligen Wahnsinn, wrapped in pleasant madness.

[30] Bündel Pfeile, sheaf of arrows. Vide Note 29, Act II. Scene 2.

beiden süßesten Freuden meines Herzens. Die göttliche Freiheit, von meiner Geliebten borgte sie die Gestalt; das reizende Mädchen kleidete sich in der Freundin himmlisches Gewand. In einem ernsten Augenblick erscheinen sie vereinigt, ernster als lieblich. Mit blutbefleckten Sohlen trat sie vor mir auf, die wehenden Falten des Saumes mit Blut befleckt. Es war mein Blut und vieler Edeln Blut. Nein, es ward nicht umsonst vergossen. Schreitet durch! Braves Volk! Die Siegesgöttin führt dich an! Und wie das Meer durch eure Dämme bricht,[31] so brecht, so reißt den Wall der Tyrannei zusammen, und schwemmt ersäufend sie von ihrem Grunde, den sie sich anmaßt, weg!

(Trommeln näher.)

Horch! Horch! Wie oft rief mich dieser Schall zum freien Schritt nach dem Felde des Streits und des Siegs! Wie munter traten die Gefährten auf der gefährlichen, rühmlichen Bahn! Auch ich schreite einem ehrenvollen Tode aus diesem Kerker entgegen; ich sterbe für die Freiheit, für die ich lebte und focht, und der ich mich jetzt leidend opfre.

(Der Hintergrund wird mit einer Reihe spanischer Soldaten besetzt, welche Hellebarden tragen.)

Ja, führt sie nur zusammen! Schließt eure Reihen, ihr schreckt mich nicht. Ich bin gewohnt, vor Speeren gegen Speere zu stehen, und, rings umgeben von dem drohenden Tod', das muthige Leben nur doppelt rasch zu fühlen.[32]

(Trommeln.)

Dich schließt der Feind von allen Seiten ein! Es blinken Schwerter; Freunde, höh'ren Muth! Im Rücken habt ihr Eltern, Weiber, Kinder!

---

[31] Meer durch eure Dämme bricht. Prophetically, alluding to the mode of warfare adopted by the Netherlands against their foreign enemies.

[32] das muthige Leben nur doppelt rasch zu fühlen, feel my courageous heart beating doubly quickly.

(Auf die Wache zeigend.)

Und diese treibt ein hohles Wort des Herrschers,[33] nicht ihr Gemüth. Schützt eure Güter! Und euer Liebstes zu erretten, fallt freudig, wie ich euch ein Beispiel gebe.

(Trommeln. Wie er auf die Wache los und auf die Hinterthür zu geht, fällt der Vorhang: die Musik fällt ein und schließt mit einer Siegessymphonie das Stück.)

---

[33] diese treibt ein hohles Wort des Herrschers, these move (in accordance with) by the empty word of the ruler.

LONDON: PRINTED BY
SPOTTISWOODE AND CO., NEW-STREET SQUARE
AND PARLIAMENT STREET